'You tw… the nurse a…

'We've met, …

'In New York …

Helen hardly dared to look him in the eye. There was an awkward pause.

'Dr Blackburn,' said Andrew in a professional tone, 'why don't we meet in the canteen for coffee, to catch up on old times?'

Helen glanced at her watch. 'I can't stay long. I have to…be somewhere soon.' She'd almost said, *I have to go home to my baby*, but stopped in time. This was definitely not the right time or place to tell Andrew that he had a baby son.

Barbara Hart was born in Lancashire and educated at a convent in Wales. At twenty-one she moved to New York, where she worked as an advertising copywriter. After two years in the USA she returned to England, where she became a television press officer in charge of publicising a top soap opera and a leading current affairs programme. She gave up her job to write novels. She lives in Cheshire and is married to a solicitor. They have two grown-up sons.

Recent titles by the same author:

ENGAGING DR DRISCOLL
A FATHER FOR HER CHILD
HER FATHER'S DAUGHTER

THE DOCTOR'S LOVE-CHILD

BY
BARBARA HART

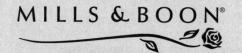

MILLS & BOON®

For Jane, Julia, Maggie and Mary

All the characters in this book have no existence outside the imagination of the author, and have no relation whatsoever to anyone bearing the same name or names. They are not even distantly inspired by any individual known or unknown to the author, and all the incidents are pure invention.

*First published in Great Britain 2002
Harlequin Mills & Boon Limited,
Eton House, 18-24 Paradise Road, Richmond, Surrey TW9 1SR*

© Barbara Hart 2002

ISBN 0 263 83086 1

*Set in Times Roman 10½ on 11¼ pt.
03-0802-43564*

*Printed and bound in Spain
by Litografía Rosés, S.A., Barcelona*

CHAPTER ONE

HELEN remembered the exact moment she'd met him. In Rolf's Deli on Sixth Avenue in midtown Manhattan.

Helen Blackburn had been so engrossed in the medical journal she'd been reading that she hadn't noticed the tall, dark-haired man in the impeccably cut suit taking his place across from her at the restaurant table. It had only been when he'd given the waitress his breakfast order that she'd glanced at him. Helen had picked up on his English accent, something of a rarity in New York.

Their eyes had met for an instant and he'd smiled at her. He was one of those people who rippled with energy and authority. She'd dropped her gaze back to the journal which she'd then lifted in order to hide behind it. A deep blush had coloured her face. You stupid woman, she'd cursed herself, pull yourself together. A handsome stranger smiles at you and you go all hot under the collar! She'd thought she'd left her blushing days well behind her, along with her gymslip and school bag. And anyway, what had she been told about getting involved with strangers in New York? Everyone back home in England had warned her about it…don't make eye contact, don't speak to strangers, all that kind of thing.

Helen had scanned the feature that she'd previously found so interesting and had continued to drink her coffee. She hadn't looked again at the man opposite but had had a distinct feeling that he'd been watching her.

'Is it good, that article you're reading?' he asked. The voice was velvety, the charm inescapable.

'Yes,' she replied curtly, keeping her eyes firmly fixed on the page.

'Are you in the medical profession?'

'Yes,' she repeated, her hands gripping the magazine tightly.

'A doctor?' the man enquired pleasantly.

'Yes.' Her voice took on a hard edge. Surely he would take the hint and realise that she didn't want to talk to him. He could be a serial killer for all she knew!

Out of the corner of her eye Helen noticed that the waitress had returned with the man's breakfast order, placing an empty mug on the table and pouring coffee for him. Helen was glad of the interruption…perhaps now the man would get the message and leave her alone.

'Wanna refill?' A pause. 'Wanna refill, ma'am?'

Helen realised with a start that the waitress was speaking to her. She was standing close by her elbow with a large pot of coffee.

'Refill? D'ya wanna refill?'

'Oh, yes, please,' said Helen. Then, realising that she needed to be leaving soon, said, 'I mean, no, thank you.'

'Make up your mind,' said the waitress, abruptly turning on her heel and walking to the next table.

Their eyes met again. Helen's and the man's.

'You've got to be quick round here,' he said, smiling broadly as he stirred non-dairy creamer into his coffee. 'No dithering.'

His smile was infectious and this time she couldn't stop herself from smiling back.

'Yes,' she said. 'You're quite right.'

She picked up her bill and took out her purse in order to pay.

'I don't mean to keep you from where you're going,' he said, 'but I couldn't help noticing the journal you were reading.'

He's trying to pick me up, thought Helen. At breakfast, for heaven's sake! An Englishman…over here on business, no doubt… A few days on his own without the wife and kiddies and he thinks he'll try his luck with me—or with any woman he decides to hit on while he's safely away from home.

'Try going to an art gallery,' she said briskly, closing the journal and stuffing it in her jacket pocket.

'Sorry?' he said, genuinely mystified by her reply.

'To pick up women. Art galleries, exhibitions, museums, that kind of place. If you want to find someone for a quick fling, no strings attached, that's where you should go. It's really quite easy to strike up conversations, or so I've been told.'

He threw back his head and guffawed loudly. Two people from the next table looked across at them.

'You've got me all wrong.' He chuckled. 'I'm not about to pounce on you!' He grinned, highly amused by the very idea. 'I was just delighted to see what you were reading. It's not my normal practice to strike up conversations with complete strangers, but, seeing you reading that particular feature, I just had to say something.'

Helen's jaw dropped. What was he going on about, sitting there grinning at her? Was he a lunatic? New York certainly had its fair share of those. Of course there were plenty of mentally disturbed people back home in Milchester—as a doctor she was acutely aware of that. But they weren't usually dressed quite so smartly and weren't quite so disarmingly good-looking as the man sitting opposite.

'I wrote it. That article on sports injuries. The one on the patellar tendon graft.'

'Oh!' said Helen in surprise.

'It gave me a real buzz, watching you become so engrossed in it.'

Seeing her amazed expression, he explained further.

'I'm Andrew Henderson. Check my name on the article if you like. And to prove I'm who I say I am, here's my card.'

He handed it to her.

She was still in a state of disbelief as she read the words DR ANDREW HENDERSON CONSULTANT ORTHOPAEDIC SURGEON.

'Nice to meet a fellow Brit,' he said, holding out his hand. 'And you are?'

'Helen Blackburn. I'm a post-doctoral student at the Sherratt Institute researching the diagnosis and treatment of sports injuries.'

'Well, well,' he said, holding her hand for a moment longer than was absolutely necessary. 'I'm connected with the Institute myself. I do a bit of lecturing there from time to time. But mainly I'm involved with the local hospital, doing clinical research. Perhaps our paths will cross at the Sherratt. I do hope so.'

'Er, yes,' she said, hurriedly rising from the table.

'I assure you I wasn't trying to pick you up.' His eyes twinkled mischievously as he added, 'Have a nice day.'

'And you, too.' Helen walked quickly to the pay desk. She couldn't wait to be out of his sight. The confrontation had made her feel extremely awkward and foolish. Imagine accusing Dr Henderson of trying to pick her up for a 'quick fling'—Dr Henderson, one of the leading specialists in the field of sports injuries!

The memory of it made her blush all over again as she strode out along Sixth Avenue in the direction of the Sherratt Institute.

After a few blocks Helen managed to put the incident in perspective, and her confidence returned. She looked up at the tall buildings as she negotiated the crowds of people on the busy pavement.

She smiled to herself with the pleasure of just being there. After seven days the novelty of it all hadn't even begun to wear off. This week, her first in Manhattan, had fulfilled all her expectations. New York was amazing and wonderful and just about everything she'd hoped it would be…and for the next six months it was going to be her home. It was the most vibrant, exciting place she had ever been, and she still couldn't get over the fact that New York looked *exactly* like it did on a postcard. She didn't know why this should come as such a surprise to her, but it did.

Milchester, where she came from, wasn't like that at all. It would be impossible to capture in a single image the former mill town in the north of England which was now a bustling cosmopolitan city.

Milchester was home to Helen—but not for the immediate future. For the next six months Dr Helen Blackburn was going to be a New Yorker—and, while she didn't want to disown her Milchester past, at present her sights were fixed on a very different skyline.

As she breezed along the pavement towards to Sherratt Institute she just couldn't believe her luck.

'Dr Blackburn, I presume,' said the smartly attired professor, standing up as Helen walked into his office. 'Alan Mulberry.' He offered his right hand in greeting, adding with smile, 'But you can call me Al, as they say in the song.'

Professor Dr Alan J Mulberry, the Institute's Director of Sports Science, was a big-framed man of medium height, whose natural bulk was kept in trim by a tight regime of diet, exercise, mineral water and will-power. His hair looked expensively groomed and, for a man in his late fifties, suspiciously dark in colour.

'I'm sorry I wasn't here on your first day at the Institute but, as you know, I was away in Australia, giving a paper at a conference on sports injuries. I hope you've been made to feel at home in our little laboratory.' He beamed at her from behind his large mahogany desk.

'Everyone's been so kind,' replied Helen. She wasn't sure whether he'd meant it for real when he'd said, 'Call me Al', or if he'd been just joking. She decided to err on the side of caution. 'And, Professor, I'd hardly call your laboratory *little*. It's absolutely enormous! Well, it certainly is compared to anything

I've ever worked in back home in England. The banks of computers, electro-microscopes, X-ray machines, scanners… And the library!'

Professor Mulberry was gratified to note how Helen's eyes shone with enthusiasm. He was duly proud of his Institute and its state-of-the-art facilities, many of which had been provided by generous patrons and sponsors.

'And your living arrangements? Did that work out OK?'

'Yes, thank you. Your secretary very kindly organised everything before I arrived over here. I'm sharing a lovely apartment a few blocks across town with another young doctor, a girl who's working in ER at the City Hospital.'

'Good,' he said. 'We want to make sure that our new post-doctoral student is well looked after, certainly one who comes with such an excellent background in orthopaedic medicine as yourself. The thesis for which you were awarded the Moreton Research Scholarship is of great interest to us here at the Sherratt Institute. You are one very bright doctor! Having you as a member of the team reflects well on all of us, I assure you, my dear. We are honoured by your presence.'

Helen looked down at the ground for a moment, temporarily embarrassed by his effusiveness.

She hadn't got used to the way some Americans had a knack of looking you straight in the eye and, without a hint of irony, heaping praise on you to your face. Back home no one in authority would have dreamt of giving such a stream of compliments to a young medic in case it went to their head and they demanded a pay rise! But here cash, or lack of it, didn't enter into the equation. It came as a pleasant surprise to Helen to find herself working in an environment where money wasn't a problem. The whole Institute reeked of it. Everything was the best that money could buy and the research facilities were the most magnificent she'd ever come across.

'I just love working here,' she said with genuine feeling.

'Are you getting on well with the other members of the team?' the professor enquired.

'Oh, yes, Professor,' replied Helen.

She was a member of an eight-person research team, all of whom were post-doctoral graduates. They were working on a sports medicine research project looking into knee injuries caused by sporting activity—in particular anterior cruciate ligament injuries.

At the centre of the research was the fact that damage to the ACL, as it was known, was one of the most common sports injuries and one of the most frequent causes of permanent disability. In England, Helen had done a lot of research on the prevention and treatment of this injury and it was this work that had been the basis for her winning the prestigious Moreton scholarship and the funding for her six months' post-doctoral research in America.

'We live in a society obsessed by sport,' said Professor Mulberry. 'We participate in it and when we're not doing it ourselves we expect it to provide us with endless entertainment. And at all levels, amateur and professional, child and adult, injury is a constant threat. And of all injuries, those to the knee represent the athlete's greatest fear and the greatest suffering. Here at the Institute we hope to do our bit towards ending that suffering. And with your help, Dr Blackburn, and a little guidance from above…' he raised his eyes heavenward '…maybe that day will come soon. Very soon, Dr Blackburn.'

Helen felt as if she'd attended a prayer meeting. She rose to leave but the professor stopped her.

'Before you go, my dear, I would just like to show you this and ask your opinion of it.' He waved a filmy object between his hands, stretching it apart and allowing it to snap back again before handing it over to her.

'It's a new type of bandage made by Perks & Perks, one of our major sponsors. As you can see, it's transparent so it doesn't put off fashion-conscious young people, and the manufacturers claim it can stop up to ninety per cent of all sports injuries to the knee.'

Helen raised her eyebrows in disbelief. 'Really?'

'Apparently so. It's something I think you should include in your research project,' announced the professor. 'I've arranged for several hundred to be sent to you for testing. Keep me informed about the test results, won't you?'

Helen left the office clutching the bandage and feeling slightly uneasy. She wasn't quite sure why, but she felt that some of the shine from her new job had begun to wear off. Perhaps all that glisters was not, after all, gold. Did her magnificent new research facilities by any chance come with strings—or bandages—attached?

* * *

Another week passed before she found herself sitting opposite Andrew Henderson again. This time it was in the Institute café.

'Mind if I join you?' he asked.

'Of course not.' She gathered up her notes to make room for his coffee-cup.

'I hope I'm not disturbing you. Are you in the middle of something?' He indicated the pile of papers she'd brought with her and which she'd been reading during her lunch-break.

'No. Nothing of importance.' She didn't explain to him that the main reason she spread out her reading material on the table was to deter Marcie, one of the laboratory technical staff, from joining her for lunch. She had latched onto Helen and made a beeline for her every time she saw her sitting quietly by herself. Marcie was a brilliant technician but the woman talked non-stop in a very squeaky, high-pitched voice.

Helen was delighted to see Andrew again. And from the beam on his face, he was just as pleased to meet her.

'So, what are you—?'

'How are you getting—?'

They both spoke at once.

'After you,' he said, taking a sip of his coffee.

'I was just wondering what you were doing in the Institute today. I remember you said you did some lecturing here.'

'I'm not actually giving a lecture today,' Andrew replied, 'but I've come in to arrange for some of my students to come and observe an operation I'm doing tomorrow…a patellar tendon graft.'

'The procedure that you wrote about in your article?'

'The very one.' He paused for a moment. 'Are you perhaps interested in coming along to the operating theatre?'

Helen jumped at the chance.

'I'd love to, Dr Henderson. It would be wonderful to have the chance of watching you operate. Reconstructing a torn knee ligament using graft tissue is something I've never had the opportunity of seeing done. I believe it's a procedure that could have a lot going for it.'

'Not Dr Henderson,' he said. 'Andrew, please.' He smiled, a warm generous smile that lit up his whole face.

'Helen.' She smiled back.

'Tell me, Helen,' he said, deliberately using her name, 'a little about your medical background. Then I'll know when not to teach my granny to suck eggs. The students I lecture are normally in their first year. I get the impression from Professor Mulberry that you are very high up in the qualifications league. Are you an MD?'

She nodded. 'After pre-registration I worked as an SHO in Milchester General while I researched a doctorate in physics. Oh, and I also took a diploma in orthopaedic surgery.'

'Phew!' said Andrew. 'No wonder you were awarded the Moreton.'

Helen returned to something he'd said earlier.

'Did you mention me to Professor Mulberry?' she asked.

'Yes, that's right.'

That's a bit blatant, thought Helen. A bit blatant but very flattering that someone as eminent as

Andrew Henderson should be interested in the medical background of a mere post-doc. student.

'Your name came up in conversation,' he replied casually. 'The professor seemed to believe that we Brits live on such a small island that we're all bound to know each other. Telling him that I had, in fact, met you only served to reinforce his belief!'

They talked for a little while longer. The minutes seemed to fly, and when they checked their watches simultaneously they each realised it was way past their time to leave.

'See you tomorrow,' he said, 'and come in time to get scrubbed up. I can always use an extra pair of hands to assist.'

That afternoon, Helen found it very difficult to concentrate on her research project for thinking about the ligament operation—and the man who would be performing it. She asked herself what was making her feel so…elated. Was it the career opportunity that was being offered to her? Or was it the prospect of seeing Andrew Henderson again and working at close quarters with him?

If she was being honest with herself…it was definitely the latter.

In the operating theatre at the orthopaedic surgery centre, Helen and Andrew faced each other over the anaesthetised body of the patient, a tall muscular young man called Delroy, an amateur basketball player who had damaged his knee three days previously.

'He's lucky to have had his condition diagnosed

and dealt with so quickly,' remarked Helen when she and Andrew were scrubbing up.

'We've found that to be crucial,' said Andrew. 'The sooner a torn ligament and damaged cartilage is diagnosed and dealt with, the higher the success rate. If there are no complications we can expect this young sportsman to return to basketball in about six months. The longer the injury is left undiagnosed and untreated, the longer it will take to cure and the greater the chance of permanent disability.'

Before he started the operation he addressed his group of students who were in a special viewing gallery, following close-ups of the proceedings on closed-circuit television.

'This young man, Delroy, presents with classic cartilage and ligament damage to his right knee as a result of a weight-bearing twist. He's a basketball player, a high-intensity activity well known for causing this type of sports injury, and his team coach said he heard a pop or snap from the knee which swelled up in a very short time. I examined him and diagnosed a badly torn ligament. Without an operation, Delroy's basketball days will, most likely, be over.'

Andrew paused for a moment before continuing.

'With this type of injury it is vital to be seen by an orthopaedic surgeon or sports injury doctor within three days. And if repair or reconstruction is required, this needs to be done within ten days of injury before soft tissue oedema creates technical difficulty. Delroy injured his knee three days ago…and now this is where Dr Blackburn and I come in.'

Helen felt herself heating up behind the surgical mask. Andrew was implying to his group of students that she was a member of his orthopaedic team—not just a hanger-on. It was a very generous act on his part and she prayed that she wasn't going to let him down.

'The operation is, as I'm sure you all know, an ACL reconstruction technique using a patellar tendon graft. In this particular procedure we will be obtaining graft tissue from the patient to replace the damaged ligament.'

Andrew glanced at Helen for a moment before looking at the inert body on the operating table.

The anaesthetist confirmed that the patient was completely anaesthetised, the gases being introduced through an endotracheal tube.

'Before we do the ACL reconstruction,' he said, speaking to his students once again, 'we will carefully survey the whole knee joint using the arthroscope.' He pointed to an instrument attached to a monitor of the type used for keyhole surgery.

'Thank you,' he said to the theatre nurse who handed him the arthroscopic probe.

Andrew and Helen scrutinised the images that appeared on the monitor as they evaluated Delroy's damaged knee. The closeness of their bodies made it seem to Helen, just for a second, that it was just the two of them in the theatre. A pulse beat in her neck.

'I'm looking to see if the meniscus cartilage is torn,' said Andrew. 'In sixty-five per cent of ACL cases we find that the meniscus is also damaged.'

He moved the probe a fraction of an inch at a time inside the knee joint before declaring, 'I think this young man is in the lucky thirty-five per cent with no damage to the meniscus, which just leaves us with the anterior cruciate ligament tear, which we can see here.' He moved the instrument in the area where he would soon be operating.

'Now we'll proceed with the main operation. Scalpel, please.' His authority was complete. No one was in any doubt as to who was in charge and all eyes were on him and his surgeon's hands.

He took the instrument handed to him by the theatre nurse and made an incision into the knee. Helen could sense the body of students moving forward in unison to get a closer look now that the first cut had been made.

'Dr Blackburn will be retracting,' Andrew informed the theatre nurse, who immediately handed Helen a retractor and swabs.

'Now that I have exposed the patellar tendon, which is here just below the skin, I'm going to remove a central strip of about ten millimetres and a small segment of bone from the patella and the tibia.'

Helen watched as Andrew, with great skill and precision, cut out two tiny pieces of bone and a strip of tendon with a special miniature drill. As he sutured the remaining portion of the patellar tendon Andrew explained to his students, and Helen, that when it had healed the patellar tendon would function normally. Then he carefully shaped the graft and prepared it for transplanting back into the knee. The harvested strip looked like a small cotton bud with pieces of bone instead of cotton wool at each end.

The operation proceeded with the damaged ligament tissues being trimmed away and the site prepared to receive the graft.

'The graft position is extremely critical,' he told

the students. 'One of the major advances in recent years is the perfection of techniques and instruments that can reliably locate and place the graft tissue literally within a millimetre of where it should go.'

Helen was totally absorbed, watching the way Andrew performed the delicate and intricate procedures with dexterity and confidence. She was also impressed by his modesty. Never once did he boast, as he could have done, that he had played a major role in developing and perfecting these very techniques.

Placing the graft correctly involved more drilling, this time to make small holes in the femur and tibia. As the sound of drilling filled the room, the kind of noise that Helen imagined the general public would probably have expected to emanate from a timber yard or a dentist's surgery, Andrew said to his students, 'There's quite a lot of this in my work. That's why we orthopaedic surgeons end up being pretty good at DIY. If anyone needs some new bookshelves put up, have a word with me after the operation.'

A ripple of laughter came from the students, and Helen behind her theatre mask let out a giggle. Andrew looked across at her, his eyes crinkling at the sides as he gave her a wink. Helen felt a warm glow spread throughout her body.

Once the holes were made, the graft was passed carefully up into the joint, with the tendon portion lying exactly where the damaged ligament used to be. The bone portions were to be fixed in place using special screws.

'We used to use metal screws,' Andrew told the students, 'but these bio-absorbable ones are much better, for obvious reasons.'

Using a medical screwdriver, Andrew fixed the two screws. He kept the probe focused inside the knee so that he and Helen could easily see when the graft had been sufficiently tightened.

Once the graft was in place he asked Helen to irrigate the joint thoroughly to make sure that all the tiny pieces of tissue and bone that might have escaped into the joint during the operation were flushed out. The skin incision was then stitched up using internal sutures to minimise scarring.

'I'm placing a small drain in the joint,' said Andrew, 'just for the first twenty-four hours. And finally,' he said to the note-taking students, 'the anaesthetist will give Delroy a measured dose of local anaesthetic into the joint…that should last six or eight hours. This is part of our pain management protocol which adds to the patient's comfort on awakening in the recovery room. It's a small detail but it makes a big difference.'

As they left the operating theatre, Helen was touched to see all the students rise and give Andrew a standing ovation.

The operation had taken two and a half hours. As they were removing their theatre garb she suddenly felt totally exhausted. It must be the tension, she told herself, standing there concentrating for all that time without a break. And if she felt like that, how must Andrew feel? She looked across at him as he stripped off his latex gloves and binned them. He seemed as fresh as the moment he'd started.

He looked up. 'Hope you found it instructive,' he said.

'I certainly did, thank you,' said Helen suppressing

a yawn. 'But I'm now totally whacked! I don't know how you manage to stay so fresh and alert, concentrating on that kind of microsurgery for hours at a time when you know that one slip could mean permanent disability for the patient.'

'You get used to it,' he said warmly. 'I actually find operating very stimulating. I just love doing it. It makes me very happy that what I do can make the world of difference to someone like Delroy. Basketball is his life and one day he hopes to play professionally.' Then, almost without pause, he asked, 'Dinner tonight, Dr Blackburn?'

CHAPTER TWO

HELEN was just out of the shower and wrapping herself in a large fluffy white bath towel when she heard the slam of her apartment door and a voice calling out, 'It's only me!'

'Oh, hi, Jane,' Helen called back. Jane Howorth and Helen shared the attractive mid-town apartment, an arrangement organised by Professor Mulberry's secretary.

'I feel wrecked,' said Jane as Helen padded out of the bathroom and into the living area. The two girls flopped down on the sofa.

'Tough day in ER?'

Jane nodded. 'A major motor vehicle accident—I believe you Brits call them road traffic accidents. Three badly injured drivers, one badly injured pedestrian. And one badly trained doggie that caused the whole messy incident.'

'Oh, dear,' said Helen, patting her friend's hand soothingly. 'Would you like me to make a cup of tea?'

Jane shook her head.

'Coffee, then? Or something stronger?'

'No, thanks, Helen. What I need straight away is what you've just had. A really long, hot shower.' She dragged herself reluctantly from the couch. 'And then we can send out for a spicy take-away and eat it watching the movie channel.'

'Ah,' said Helen, suddenly feeling guilty. 'I'm going out for dinner. We'll do the take-away tomorrow, shall we?'

'No problem,' said Jane, making her way to the bathroom. 'Going anywhere nice?'

'Not sure. He didn't mention where we'd eat.'

Jane paused in the doorway. 'So. Who is he? This man who's taking you heaven knows where?'

Helen turned her head away slightly in an effort to appear casual. 'Dr Henderson.'

Jane gave a long, low whistle. 'Nice work, Dr Blackburn. I guess your eyes met over that patellar tendon and, wham, it was a done deal, huh?'

Helen couldn't help but laugh at the comical way Jane had exaggerated her Midwest accent as she said that last sentence.

'I suppose you could say that's what happened!' Helen chortled. 'Maybe he liked the way I assisted at the operation. Either that or he wants to talk to someone from home.'

Jane looked impressed. 'You assisted? That's great! I knew he'd asked you to come and watch, but it's a surprise to find you were invited to assist.'

'It was a surprise to me,' replied Helen. 'A very nice surprise. I feel I've learned such a lot today.'

'Lucky you,' said Jane. 'And I don't just mean for assisting at the operation. Lucky you for going out with Dr Gorgeous.'

'I'd forgotten that you'd met him.'

'Quite a few times,' replied Jane. 'He's often around the ER, doing his clinical research. We all think he's great. But as far as I know he's never asked one of us out on a date!'

Helen plugged in the hairdryer and began to blow-dry her shoulder-length hair. 'Perhaps he just wants to discuss the operation,' she said.

'Maybe.' Jane winked, adding, 'Take your note-book,' before disappearing into the bathroom.

Helen gave careful consideration to what she should wear for the dinner date.

Wanting to look dressy but not over-dressed, she took a great amount of care and attention to detail. It involved the trying on and rejection of several outfits before she finally settled on the right combination. She groomed her dark, lustrous hair into a freshly windswept look, a style that made her mother always say, 'Why don't you put a neat parting in your hair and brush it smooth?' Most other days she wouldn't have been bothered to spend all that time on getting ready, but tonight was different…tonight was special.

At least she hoped it was going to be. As Andrew arrived to pick her up, she slipped a notebook into her handbag…just in case.

The effort she had put into her appearance had, gratifyingly, not gone unnoticed by Andrew. His eyes swept over her approvingly.

'You look just perfect for where I have in mind,' he said.

Flagging down a cab outside the apartment block, he instructed the driver to take them to an address in mid-town Manhattan.

'I hope you don't suffer from vertigo,' said Andrew, 'because we're going to a very high restau-rant, The Big Window.'

The cab dropped them off at a building which

loomed high above the city. They walked through the lobby and rode the non-stop lift to the top floor, a vertical trip which took almost a minute.

'You *don't* get vertigo, do you?' said Andrew, suddenly becoming concerned. 'I suppose I should have checked with you before. This place is a quarter of a mile up in the sky with floor-to-ceiling windows and—'

'I have no problem with heights.' Helen laughed, seeing the stricken look on his face. 'My grandfather was a steeplejack so it must be in the genes. I also did a fair bit of mountaineering in my teens.'

'Terrific,' said Andrew. 'In that case, you can hold my hand while I creep up to the edge of the windows. Even though I know the glass is there and that it's hellish thick, looking down over that sheer drop can be more than a little daunting. When I came here previously I had to stand back a foot and brace my hands against the window-frames!'

Even though Helen had come prepared for a very, very high view, when they entered the bar and she looked out of the enormous glass panels that took the place of two of the outer walls, she couldn't stop herself from gasping.

Andrew had booked a table next to the window and facing north. 'This place has one of the best views in New York,' he told her as they were directed across the restaurant.

The panorama was spectacular, taking in the vertical strips of the Manhattan avenues, the Empire State Building, the Hudson River and the George Washington Bridge. They spent the first few minutes pointing and identifying the city landmarks.

'There's the Chrysler Building.'

'What's that strange-looking building over there, the one near the white one with spires?'

'Is that the Sherratt Institute, over to the left of that building with a roof garden?'

'There's my apartment building!'

Sipping a glass of chilled white wine and gazing out over the breathtaking view, Helen sighed contentedly. 'I feel as if I've just died and gone to heaven!'

'It is pretty heavenly, I agree,' said Andrew as he ran a finger down the bare flesh of her arm.

At that moment the waiter came to take their order and after that the conversation moved away from romantic venues to a more down-to-earth topic.

'How did you first come to be interested in sports medicine?' Andrew asked.

'I suppose it's because I've always been a sporty person,' she replied. 'Junior athlete at school, a short burst at gymnastics and later on being a mad tennis fiend. I'd even considered being a professional sports person…an athletics coach or tennis teacher…but I was also keen to be a doctor. My late father was a GP and I grew up believing that's what I would most probably do. So a job that combined sports and medicine seemed the ideal choice. How about you?'

'An almost identical scenario,' he replied. 'But I also suffered a sports injury in my college years—a pulled hamstring—and it was while I was being treated for it that, like you, I realised I could have a job that involved medicine and sport, both of which I loved. Still do.'

Andrew paused for a moment and lightly stroked

his finger across her arm again. 'Have you brought your tennis racket with you?'

Helen was startled. 'Tonight?'

Andrew threw back his head and laughed out loud, a rich, warm sound that reminded her of their first meeting in Rolf's Deli. 'No, not tonight!' he said.

'Oh, I see what you mean,' replied Helen. 'Did I bring it with me to New York? Yes, I did. The trouble is, I'm not sure where or when I'll get to play.'

'My club,' he said decisively. 'I hereby challenge you to a match.'

'That'd be great,' enthused Helen. 'I could certainly do with the exercise. I'm trying to find time to get to a gym as well. Professor Mulberry tells me there's one near the Institute where we have a special arrangement.'

'That's the one I'm a member of,' said Andrew. 'It's very convenient for those art galleries you were telling me about.'

The words didn't sink in at first. 'Art galleries?' Then the penny dropped as she recalled her embarrassment at accusing him of trying to pick her up for a quick fling.

'Not making you blush, am I?' He grinned wickedly at her.

As the evening progressed their conversational chat became more serious…and intimate. She noticed how frequently he was touching her, fleeting butterfly caresses on her hand and arm…touches that sent thrills through her each time they made contact, flesh on flesh. And his eyes, gazing deeply into hers, spoke volumes about his future intentions. Jane had been wrong. The last thing Helen would be doing tonight was taking notes about the patellar tendon graft.

After the meal they walked a few blocks hand in hand in the warm night air before stopping a cab. Andrew climbed into the back seat next to her and, sliding his arm round her shoulders, pulled her to him and kissed her. A kiss so wonderful that for the second time that evening Helen thought she might have died and gone to heaven.

It was a whole week before Helen met up with Andrew again. A whole week that she spent wondering if he would ask her out again or if that one date had been all they would ever share.

'Perhaps he just asked me out as a kind of thank you for assisting at the operation?' she suggested to Jane. 'Maybe it wasn't a proper date after all.'

'He's very busy at the hospital. I know that because I've seen him around nearly every day.' Jane was making cinnamon toast for the two of them. 'He's real cute, isn't he?'

'Just a bit.'

'More than just a bit, I'd say.' Jane handed her the toast.

'You're right,' admitted Helen. 'He's the most gorgeous man I've met in ages.' She bit into the toast. 'Wait till I tell the folks back home about this.'

'About Dr Henderson?'

'About cinnamon toast. We've never heard of it in Milchester!'

The following day, Helen scanned the tables in the Institute café as she had been doing, fruitlessly, all week. This time her heart gave a lurch as she noticed

Andrew sitting alone at a table in the corner, his head buried in a book.

She was about to take her lunch tray over to join him when her courage failed her. She couldn't bring herself to do it. What if Andrew had been deliberately avoiding her? If that was the case, it could turn out embarrassing…she certainly didn't want to appear as if she was chasing him. But on the other hand he might think *she* was ignoring him. It was hard being a woman even in these liberated times!

She compromised by waving to him when he looked up temporarily from his book and putting her tray down at another table where one of her post-doc. colleagues was sitting. He was called Ken and his speciality was tennis elbow. He'd informed her that Ken was short for Kensington—and was mildly offended when her automatic reaction to this information had been to burst out laughing.

She and Ken were deep in conversation—some gossip he'd heard about the professor—when Helen was touched gently on the shoulder. Turning round, she looked into the brown eyes of Andrew Henderson.

'If you'll excuse me,' he said courteously to Helen's lunch companion, 'I'd like a quick word with Helen.'

'Sure,' said Ken. 'I'm just going to refresh my coffee-cup.'

'Please, stay,' said Andrew. 'It's not a private conversation.'

Ken had slid out from the bench seat. 'I need another injection of caffeine so, please, be my guest, Dr Henderson.'

As Andrew moved into the seat vacated by Ken, Helen experienced a pang of disappointment. Not a private conversation, he'd said. So he wasn't about to ask her out on another date!

'Hi,' she said, giving him her most winning smile.

'Hi. I was wondering if you could spare me some of your time later on this afternoon?'

'Sure,' she said, trying to sound casual as her heart rate went racing.

'I'm giving a paper at a medical conference next month. I was wondering…well, hoping actually…that I could persuade you to collaborate on it with me.'

She was completely taken aback.

'Me? Collaborate with you?'

'Why not? I find your ideas stimulating and your avenues of knee-injury research innovative and re-freshing. I'd be most grateful for your input.'

Her pulse was hammering away and her mouth had gone dry. She took a sip of water before answering.

'That's…that's very flattering,' she said. 'I'd be de-lighted to collaborate with you. Just tell me how and when.'

'I've a class of students this afternoon but I'll be finished about five o'clock. Can we meet then?'

She nodded.

'Good,' he said, getting up as Ken arrived back at the table. 'I'll come down to the lab for you and we'll find somewhere quiet.'

When Andrew had left Ken looked knowingly at Helen. 'A date with the handsome doctor?'

'Work,' said Helen briskly, before changing the subject.

*   *   *

The afternoon dragged on. Helen found herself checking her watch every ten minutes. Just before five, Andrew came into the lab.

'Can you bring as much material as possible?' he said. 'We might need it for reference purposes. I promise you'll get the credit for anything I use that's yours.'

'I never doubted it for a minute,' she said, gathering her papers together and dropping them into her document case.

'There's a small meeting room on the fifth floor. I've reserved it for us,' he said as they walked to the lift. 'I hope you don't mind giving up some of your free time.'

'I don't mind at all,' she replied, attempting to sound cool. If only he knew how absolutely, totally delighted she was!

When the lift arrived there were four people already inside. Helen and Andrew had to stand very close to each other, very close indeed…a sensation Helen found remarkably pleasurable.

In the meeting room they sat on opposite sides of the conference table, spreading their various papers over its shiny surface.

They worked on the project for nearly two hours, taking one short break for refreshments. Andrew had used his considerable charm to negotiate for a jug of iced tea and a plate of cookies to be brought up to the room by a café assistant even though the café was now technically closed for the evening.

'Would you be happy to present the paper with me?' he asked when they'd finished work for the day.

'I'm not sure,' she admitted.

'Nervous about the prospect of speaking to a large gathering of medics? It can be a bit daunting the first time.'

Helen pondered for a moment.

'I've made presentations before,' she said. 'Not on such a large scale, I must admit. The reason I'm hesitating is that I don't want to appear to be muscling in on your platform. It might look as if I'm trying to grab some of your glory.'

'Well,' said Andrew, 'I don't want to put you in an awkward position if that's what's worrying you. There's a lot of jealousy out there, I know. But in your case you would be entitled to grab some of the glory, as you put it. Your ideas, particularly in relation to non-operative treatments for sports injuries, are particularly thought-provoking. But it's entirely up to you, Helen. I won't push you into the limelight. Not yet anyway. But think about it.'

Having promised she'd do just that, Andrew suggested they go and grab a pizza.

'My stomach's rumbling,' he said as they entered the Pizza Perfect restaurant on the same block as the Institute. Secretly Helen had been hoping that when he'd suggested a pizza he'd meant a take-away or one that would be delivered to his apartment. She didn't want to rush things with Andrew—and chance would be a fine thing—but a cosy evening over at his place sharing a pizza and a couple of beers sounded very appealing to her.

Over a large-sized house-special pizza the conversation turned once again to the medical conference that would be taking place in New York the following month and would be attended by delegates from all over the world.

'The more I think about it,' said Helen, cutting herself a second slice, 'the more I think I'd like you to present the paper on your own, with me sitting in the auditorium. For this first time, anyway.'

'This first time?' repeated Andrew. 'Do I take it you're open to persuasion to collaborate on another occasion?'

'If you'd like me to…and you don't think I'm being too pushy.'

'Not pushy—ambitious,' he said, smiling at her in that way she found irresistible. 'And, believe me, there's nothing wrong with ambition. I suffer from it myself.'

They shared a taxi home after their meal and, as on the previous occasion, he kissed her before dropping her off at her apartment block.

Helen couldn't figure Andrew out. His kisses were those of a lover, but he behaved more like a friend. Not even that sometimes…more a colleague. She could still feel the tantalising touch of his lips on hers. It felt good…it turned her on, and it made her realise that she wanted more from this relationship. Much more.

It had been a busy day in the laboratory. Assisted by Marcie, Helen had been analysing some new data gathered from the casualty departments of New York hospitals. They'd sifted through the material, picking out all the significant knee injuries over a twelve-month period.

At four o'clock, when she was considering taking a break, her phone rang. It was Andrew.

'Are you doing anything after work?' he asked. Her heart gave a small leap. Was he going to ask her out on a date?

'Nothing much,' she replied. 'What did you have in mind? Something to do with the conference?'

'Not this time,' he said. 'You remember Delroy, the young man we did the knee graft on?'

How could she forget? It had been the high point of her medical career to date.

'Of course. Is everything going well with him?'

'Come and see for yourself,' he said. 'That's why I'm phoning. I'm going to call in on him this evening to check on his progress. As you took a hand in the operation I thought you might like to join me.'

Helen jumped at the chance. 'Oh, yes, please. That would be great. I'm very keen to see things through.' Particularly with you...

As she put down the phone she was smiling. She was absolutely thrilled that Andrew was including her in his post-operative work. Slowly the smile turned to a sigh when it hit her that Andrew hadn't been, as she'd first expected, phoning to ask her out on a date.

She met him, as arranged, by the front steps of the Institute and they hailed a taxi. When Andrew gave the cabbie the address the man grumbled and muttered something about 'just my luck'.

'I'll make it worth your while,' she heard Andrew tell him.

'What's the matter with him?' she asked.

'He's not keen on going up there. It's not the most salubrious part of Manhattan.'

As they drove north, leaving behind them the famous landmark buildings, Helen noticed the subtle way, block by block, the apartment buildings and shops became more shabby and less cared for. There were also fewer people out on the streets, giving the areas they were driving through an underlying air of menace. Helen shivered involuntarily.

'Such a big change in such a relatively short distance,' said Andrew, picking up on her unspoken thoughts. 'How the other half lives.'

'Mmm,' responded Helen. 'I was just thinking…it reminded me of parts of Milchester. The buildings aren't as tall as here, of course, but the deprivation is just as bad…just as grim.'

The cab pulled up outside a bleak-looking tenement. The moment Andrew had paid him the cabbie switched off his 'for hire' sign and set off at speed.

'It's people like Delroy that make my job worthwhile,' said Andrew as they walked up the four flights of rubbish-strewn stairs. 'Being a good athlete is often the only chance someone like him has of escaping from all this. He's well on the way to being a professional basketball player and this injury could have ended it all for him…and ended his hopes of getting a better life.'

They rang the doorbell. It was answered by Delroy.

'Hello, Dr Henderson,' he said, smiling broadly.

'Delroy, this is Dr Blackburn, who assisted me at your operation.'

'Please, come in, both of you.'

They walked behind the tall young man into the apartment. He was limping slightly, keeping one leg stiff.

'I see you're managing without the crutches,' said Andrew as they followed him into the living room. An older woman was sitting in a shabby armchair.

'Yes, Doctor, I'm doing real good, aren't I, Momma?'

Andrew went over to the woman who was struggling to get up. 'Pleased to meet you, Mrs Johnson.' He offered his hand before adding, 'Can I help you up?'

'Momma has this real bad hip,' Delroy explained. He and Andrew helped Mrs Johnson out of her seat.

'I keep telling Delroy he shouldn't be lifting me like this, not with his bad knee. You tell him, Doctor. Maybe he'll listen to you!'

'As long as he takes the weight on his good leg, there's no reason for you to worry about that, Mrs Johnson.'

Delroy's mother straightened up and stood next to her son, who towered over her. 'While you two doctors talk to Delroy I'm going to make you all a jug of my special coffee. I grind the beans myself and the blend is my own secret recipe.' She hobbled stiffly across the room and out into the kitchen.

Helen spoke to Delroy with concern. 'Your mother's hip seems very bad. Can't she get anything done about it?'

'The hospital says she needs a hip replacement,' said Delroy, 'but they don't say when that will be. And she hasn't got the insurance for it. So…' he shrugged '…I was saving up for her, but this knee injury put back my chances of a professional career.'

'Only by six months,' said Andrew reassuringly. 'That is, if you're following my instructions to the letter…keeping up with the rehab programme and not rushing into any sporting activity.'

'I sure am, Doc,' said Delroy with gusto. 'And my coach is making sure of it, too. I've followed everything you've said. I'm not risking my future career on the short term.'

'Excellent.' Andrew patted him on the shoulder in a gesture of solidarity. 'Now, let's recap on what's happened so far in your rehab schedule. How soon were you able to walk without pain?'

'About one week. Something like that.'

'Without crutches?'

'I kept using one of them for a few more days and then I went without it.'

'And can you now lift the leg without assistance when you're lying on your back?'

'Sure thing. I'll give you a demo.' Delroy lay down on the threadbare carpet and slowly elevated his leg.

Helen turned to Andrew. 'That's astonishing after the bad injury he had to his knee.'

'It's a very successful operation,' said Andrew, 'but only if the patient looks after the knee properly in the crucial weeks afterwards.' Andrew helped Delroy to get up from the floor. 'What about the leg immobiliser?' he asked.

'I still have that, but I'm due to take it off any day now.'

'Why not now?' suggested Andrew. 'You have two doctors in attendance, so make the most of the opportunity!'

Andrew and Helen removed the leg brace and examined the knee. It was healing well and there was very little swelling in evidence.

A few minutes later, Mrs Johnson came into the room, carrying a coffee-pot.

'Hey, Momma, let me do that!' Delroy attempted to get up quickly but Andrew put a restraining hand on him. 'I'll get it, Delroy. Remember what I said about avoiding sudden movements, especially now that you've had the leg brace removed.'

Helen had also reacted quickly and relieved Mrs Johnson of the heavy coffee-pot.

'It makes me so mad,' fumed Mrs Johnson, 'being a cripple like this!'

'It's going to be all right, Momma,' said Delroy, deep frustration clouding his eyes. 'When I'm better I'm going to make that money real quick for your operation. Just you see if I don't.'

CHAPTER THREE

THE tennis ball came flying over the net like a bullet. With great effort Helen managed to reach it before it did a second bounce and flicked it back to Andrew. He returned it to her with the force of a missile.

She missed.

'Hey,' she said crossly. 'This is supposed to be a friendly, not Wimbledon centre court!'

Andrew laughed. 'Just getting rid of a bit of aggression.'

'Well, can we have a knock up first?' she said. 'Or you're going to be playing on your own!'

He lobbed another ball gently in her direction. 'I like it when you get cross and show me your feisty side. It reminds me of when we first met!'

Hitting the ball to and fro over the net, Helen began to relax and enjoy the game, although she was finding it hard to concentrate on her tennis technique. The sight of Andrew in his tennis shorts was quite a distraction, the dazzling white emphasising the golden tan of his long, athletic legs. It took a great effort on her part to keep her mind on her forehand and backhand.

'You're not a bad player,' conceded Andrew when she took the first game off him. 'I'm beginning to regret giving you such a favourable handicap!'

There was a twinkle in his eyes as they changed ends, and she blushed suddenly, too aware of his admiring glance as it swept over her slim figure dressed in the rather short tennis dress she'd borrowed from Jane.

'I was the tennis captain at school,' she said quickly to cover her embarrassment at his scrutiny, then she laughed. 'Did you think I'd be a walk-over, then?'

'Yes,' he admitted, smiling at her as they passed each other. For a second their eyes locked and Helen felt a crackle of intense attraction dart through her.

It was a month since the sports medicine conference and the paper that Andrew had presented had gone well. Many of the delegates had congratulated him on the work and Andrew, in turn, had introduced them to Helen as the joint author. She'd met so many of the top people in sports medicine and Orthopaedics at the conference that she'd almost been overwhelmed.

In the weeks following the conference she hadn't seen a lot of Andrew. He'd been away from New York on some days and extremely busy the rest of the time. When he'd suggested the game of tennis she'd been a little ambivalent about accepting. She was finding it very hard to come to terms with their relationship…if she could call it that. Sometimes it felt more like a non-relationship. Her feelings for him were growing stronger by the minute, but she was very unsure of how *he* felt about *her*. On the rare occasions they were alone together he appeared to find her attractive. She could tell by the way he touched her, the way he looked at her, the way he kissed her…but maybe that was just Andrew, maybe that was his way with every woman.

After the game, which he just managed to win, they showered at the tennis club. When they'd changed into jeans and sweatshirts, Andrew made a suggestion.

'We could leave our tennis gear here while we have a bite to eat. Shall we do that?'

She hesitated. Was she letting herself in for a little more heartache by accepting? When she'd agreed to play tennis she'd told herself that it was purely for the exercise. She had no intention of letting him raise her hopes only for them to be dashed.

'Are you working tonight?' he asked when she didn't answer immediately.

She shook her head. 'I'm not working.' All her resolve melted. 'Yes, let's get a bite to eat.'

'I know a great little Mexican place round the corner,' he said, putting an arm round her and walking her out of the door. 'Do you like fajitas?'

'Yes,' she replied. She could have added, I'd eat cardboard if it's with you.

Sitting opposite Andrew in the restaurant, Helen flicked a glance across at him as he studied the menu. Just what was it with this man? She'd known him for several weeks now and had discovered that he was kind, generous, good fun. But just what was his background, what made him tick? More importantly, why did she get the feeling he was holding back on her? She had to find out more about Andrew Henderson to dispel the image that had formed in her mind that he was man of mystery with secrets in his life. She went for the most obvious explanation of his attitude towards her.

'Are you married or anything?' she asked when they were at the coffee stage.

He shook his head, grinning mischievously. 'Not even "anything". How about you?'

'No.'

They sat in silence for a minute or two before Helen could summon up enough courage to question him further.

'Where in England do you come from?'

'Norfolk,' he replied.

'I love Norfolk,' Helen enthused. 'My father used to take me sailing on the Broads when I was young. Do you still have family connections there?'

He didn't answer straight away, drinking his coffee slowly before replying. 'I own a house in the small village where I grew up. It's empty at the moment and I'm considering selling it.'

Helen could sense that the light atmosphere between them had darkened.

He continued. 'Both my parents are dead. My mother most recently, about eighteen months ago.'

'I'm sorry,' said Helen. 'When did your father die?'

'Many, many years ago,' said Andrew looking into the distance as if remembering another lifetime.

'You once told me that he was a doctor—or at least when I said that my late father had been a GP you seemed to imply a similar scenario.'

He dipped his head in acknowledgement but said nothing.

'I was only twelve when my father died,' Helen said. 'My mother married again. I get on really well with my stepfather.' She wondered why she was volunteering all this unasked-for information about her-self when her sole intention in instigating the con-versation was to find out more about Andrew. She asked him, 'How old were you when your father died?'

He paused before answering, as if he was calculat-ing…as though this was something he hadn't thought of in years. 'About eighteen or nineteen. Something like that. The whole thing had gone on for so long that it's hard to remember when he actually died. He'd been like a dead man for quite some time before his actual death.'

'A long illness?'

'No. Just a long and very messy confrontation.'

Helen raised her eyebrows. 'Did somebody hit him?'

His voice took on a bitter tone. 'Might just as well have done. That would have been a cleaner way of killing him. Instead of which, a female patient falsely accused him of sexual impropriety. He denied it, of course, and at a court hearing he was vindicated. But by then he was a broken man. He had a nervous breakdown with the strain and never practised medi-cine again. He was old before his time and just faded away. The death certificate said it was heart failure but as far as I'm concerned it was murder.'

'How terrible,' she whispered, reaching across the table and touching his hand. 'That's a tragic way to end a life. What happened to the woman who made the allegation?'

'I have no idea. I just remember her face when my father was pronounced not guilty. She laughed and shrugged her shoulders. No doubt she moved to another town and tried the same trick on some other innocent GP.'

'I wonder what her motive was in doing that to your father? What could she possibly hope to have gained?'

'Money. She was trying to blackmail him. *Pay up or I'll say we're having an affair.*'

He turned her hand round, enfolding it in his. 'It's not a time of my life I care to remember, so let's talk about something more cheerful. There's another sports medicine conference on the horizon. In June, in Seattle.'

'Seattle. That's nice. Actually,' she admitted, 'I'm not even sure where that is. Is it near Los Angeles or over there somewhere?'

He smiled a slow smile as he could see her struggling mentally with the geography of the United States.

'Yes, Helen, it's "over there somewhere". On the west coast but much more north than LA. Close to the Canadian border.'

'Hmmm,' she mused. 'That's a long way to go for a day's conference.'

'It takes place over a weekend,' he explained. 'I was wondering if you would come and present "our" paper with me?'

Helen stared at him. 'Oh, wow!' She thought for a moment. 'Do you think I could? I mean, what about the professor? Do you suppose he'd mind me taking time off from my work at the Institute? It was only one day for the New York conference, but *Seattle*...'

Andrew laughed. 'You make it sound as if it's on

another planet! It's a conference. You wouldn't miss much time at the Institute.'

As they stepped out of the restaurant a little later, Andrew's mobile phone rang.

'Sorry about this,' he apologised to Helen as he answered the call.

They continued walking along the street as Andrew had a short conversation with his caller. He switched off the phone and replaced it in the pocket of his jeans.

'That was good news,' he said, taking hold of her hand as they made their way towards the building that housed the tennis club. 'You remember Delroy's mother?'

'The poor woman who needs a hip replacement?'

'That was the hospital. They're fitting her in as an emergency and she'll be first on my list tomorrow morning.'

'That's wonderful news!' exclaimed Helen. 'How did you manage that?'

'Better not to ask,' he said, putting a finger to his lips.

'I bet you pulled a few strings, didn't you?'

'The woman is in genuine medical need of the operation. That's all anybody needs to know.'

They strolled along in the warm summer air, holding hands. She felt calm and happy…he had that effect on her.

'When your six months' research is up, are you planning on staying?' he asked out of the blue.

The question made her stomach bunch into a tight knot. He wanted to know about her plans for the future. Could that mean he was interested in whether or not she stayed in America? It was something she had been considering quite seriously and had discussed the possibilities with Jane on several occasions.

'I think I might,' she told him cautiously. 'In the short term, anyway. There are a lot of American-based jobs in sports medicine advertised in the medical journals. Many more than in the UK. It could be a good career move to work here for a year or so.'

Andrew squeezed her hand but made no comment.

'What do you think?' she probed. 'Do you think I should stay?'

'It's entirely up to you,' he said, 'but, like you, I believe it would be good for your career. Of course, with a medical background like yours you have a very promising future wherever you choose to work.'

She was stung by his reply. Stung and disappointed. She'd been hoping that his motive in asking her whether she was staying in the US had been to establish whether or not she could be around for him on a personal level but all he'd done had been to focus on her medical career. Well, she mustn't read too much into it—at least he'd asked her to go along with him to the Seattle conference. A weekend away with him might be just the thing to kick-start a romance.

As they walked up the steps of the tennis club they were confronted by three people, two men and a woman, in their tennis clothes. Andrew recognised one of the men, a New York lawyer with whom he'd played the occasional game.

'Andrew!' said the lawyer, 'thank heavens you're here. The doorman said you'd be coming back to collect your things—'

'Tim!' interrupted the other man. 'Tell him about Mary, for heavens' sake!'

'I'm getting there,' said Tim, who was obviously doing things in his own time. 'It's Mary, my wife. She did something to her wrist while we were having a game. She didn't fall over or anything—she just hit the ball very gently, as far as I could see, and then she screamed out in agony…'

'Where is she now?' Andrew asked.

'In the locker room,' said the woman who was with them.

Helen and Andrew followed the three tennis-club members into the locker room where a woman, pale-faced with pain, was sitting stiffly upright in a cane chair holding her right arm against her chest. The other woman went over to her and said soothingly, 'There's a doctor here, Mary. Tim knows him.'

'There are two doctors here, actually,' said Andrew, going over to the patient. 'My colleague, Dr Blackburn, is also a medic.'

He bent down next to the woman who appeared to be in great pain. 'Tell me what happened,' he said gently.

'That's just it,' she said, still clutching her right arm. 'I have no idea what happened. We were playing tennis, just a slow knock-up because I haven't played for some time. I hit the ball over the net and at that same moment I heard this sickening crack…or maybe I just felt it go crack, I'm not sure. But I think I've broken my wrist. Sounds impossible, I know, from such a little thing.'

'Are you in a lot of pain?' Andrew asked, checking that she wasn't bleeding from the injury.

'It's not too bad now,' she replied, 'not as painful as when it happened. But I wouldn't mind having a painkiller…Tim was going to get me some ibuprofen from the drugstore down the street.'

'It's better if you take nothing orally for now,' said Andrew, 'in case you need a general anaesthetic to reset the bone.'

As he was talking he was making a tentative examination of Mary's arm and wrist, moving the injured area as little as possible but noting that her hand was fixed at an unnatural angle and that the area around the suspected fracture was swollen and red. He turned to Helen, who was standing beside him. 'Colles' fracture. Do you agree?'

'It certainly seems the most likely diagnosis,' she confirmed, 'from the way the wrist has been pushed back over the broken bone.'

Helen spoke to Mary. 'Are you sure you didn't also fall over and put your hand out to save yourself? That's the most usual way of doing something like this to your wrist.'

'I didn't fall,' said Mary. 'That's what's so puzzling. I wouldn't have been too surprised if I'd been an old lady with osteoporosis, but I'm only in my thirties! Ouch!' she exclaimed. 'It's agony when I move it!'

'What we need to do, Mary,' said Andrew, 'is to immobilise the whole arm until we get you to hospital. That will reduce the pain and prevent further injury. Now, what can we use for a splint?' he said, casting his eyes hopefully around the locker room.

Helen searched the room and found some thick pieces of cardboard stacked in one corner. 'Here's some discarded packaging from a pair of tennis shoes,' she said. 'It's nice and clean.'

'That'll do fine,' said Andrew, who was at that moment raiding the first-aid cabinet. He pulled out packages of cotton wool, gauze dressing and rolled bandages. Working together, he and Helen placed the cardboard splint, padded with the cotton wool and gauze bandages, under the injured lower arm. They held the improvised splint in place with more gauze bandages, checking Mary's pulse and temperature to ensure that the splint hadn't been applied too tightly.

They made a sling from a large square of blue fabric that Tim mysteriously produced.

'That looks familiar,' said his tennis companion.

'It's from one of the tables in the club dining room,' replied Tim matter-of-factly.

Mary, even though she was still in some pain, gasped at his audacity. 'You mean you tore up one of those damask tablecloths to make a sling for me? What will the club secretary say?'

Tim was unrepentant. 'The massive subs I pay to this club entitle me to rip up the occasional tablecloth from time to time. It's not the Turin shroud, for Pete's sake!'

That made Mary laugh for the first time since the accident.

'You're obviously feeling a little better,' said Andrew. 'Is the pain subsiding?'

'Much better,' she replied. 'Just taking the weight off it seems to have helped enormously…and keeping it immobilised like this.'

'Good,' said Andrew. 'We'll get you to hospital

now. Can Tim drive you there or should we call a taxi?'

'I'll drive,' said her husband. 'My car's parked in the basement.'

'Here's the address for City Hospital,' said Andrew, scribbling it down on a piece of scrap paper. 'I'll phone my colleague in Orthopaedics and tell him to expect you.' He turned to Helen. 'Is Jane on duty today?' Helen confirmed that she was. 'Excellent. We'll also put a call through to Dr Jane Howorth in the ER.'

'What will they do, do you think?' Mary asked.

'Before attempting to reset it, they'll obviously need X-rays to get a clear picture of the type of fracture and the degree of displacement, then the setting will most likely be done under an anaesthetic. At some point they may want to do a bone scan to check whether the fracture is pathological due to osteoporosis.'

'You gotta be kidding!' exclaimed Mary. 'I'm thirty-eight, not eighty-three! I'm way too young for all that fragile bones stuff.' She raised her eyebrows in disbelief. 'Aren't I?'

'I would have thought so,' confirmed Andrew. 'But it's a possibility. It's quite rare and unusual, but younger people, some very young, can also suffer from osteoporosis. In all likelihood you won't have it—the bone scan is just to rule that out.'

When Tim and Mary were safely on their way to the hospital and Andrew and Helen had picked up their sports bags ready to make their way home, Andrew touched her lightly on the arm.

'So, are you coming with me? I'd like to know so I can make plans.'

'Where to?' Helen asked, genuinely puzzled.

'Seattle—to the conference. Are you game for it?' He slipped his arm round her and nuzzled his face against hers, whispering in her ear, 'You won't regret it, I promise you.' Her heart began to race out of control before he added, 'It will look terrific on your CV.'

CHAPTER FOUR

'HI, MUM, it's me. I'm phoning from Seattle.'

'Helen! How lovely to hear from you.' Her mother's voice was husky.

'Are you all right, Mum? You sound a little groggy.'

'So would you if you'd been phoned in the middle of the night!'

Helen gave a short gasp. 'I'd forgotten about the extra time difference. I was working it out on a New York time scale. Sorry.'

'Don't apologise, love. I wouldn't miss one of your phone calls for all the world.' Her voice now sounded more awake and normal. 'So tell me about Seattle. Is the conference going well?'

'Fantastic,' enthused Helen. 'Both Seattle and the conference. I'm looking out of my hotel window across the Puget Sound and to the islands in the bay…it's just so beautiful. You'd love it. I'll treat you to a trip over here one day. One day when I'm work-ing and earning decent money in sports medicine. And that shouldn't be too far off. I've made some marvellous contacts here at the conference. I've even had a couple of job offers, which I'm seriously con-sidering.'

There was a pause. A silence from the other end of the line.

'Are you still there, Mum?'

'Yes, love. That's really great news. About the job offers.'

Helen sensed a tension, an anxiety in her mother's voice.

'You don't mind, do you?' she asked. 'You don't mind me working in America for a little while? I know I haven't mentioned it before, but I wasn't sure whether I'd actually be able to get work over here, even though Andrew assured me that I would.'

'Andrew?'

'I told you about Andrew, didn't I? The orthopaedic surgeon who asked me to assist at one of his knee operations, the person I'm presenting the paper with at the conference.'

'Oh, Dr Henderson?'

'Yes, that's the one.'

Her mother gave a low chuckle. 'This Andrew seems to be playing a big role in your life at the moment. Do I detect more than a professional relationship between you two?'

Helen sighed. 'I know it sounds silly, but I'm not really sure. I'd certainly like it to be more than just a professional relationship, but Andrew is a bit of a mystery man. I never know what his thoughts are on that subject.'

'Would you say he's playing hard to get? I've met one or two like that in my time. We used to call them confirmed bachelors…until they met that special woman and then they fell hook, line and sinker.'

'Maybe that's it,' mused Helen. 'I'll just have to zoom in on him and make him realise that I'm that special woman!'

'I should think so!' said her mother emphatically.

'In my completely biased opinion you're so special that I doubt there's a man on this earth good enough for you. And Jack feels the same way! You know that your stepfather couldn't be prouder of you if you were his own daughter.'

Tears stung Helen's eyes. The conversation was getting a little on the emotional side, reminding her that, no matter how far she travelled following the rapidly rising star of her medical career, homesickness was never too far below the surface.

'You don't mind, do you?' she asked again, trying to keep her voice on an even keel. 'You don't mind if I work in New York for a year or so instead of coming straight home when my Moreton scholarship ends?'

'Of course not!' emphasised her mother. 'You're young and brilliant, with the world at your feet. You must do exactly what you want to do, my darling daughter, and don't be worrying about us back home in Milchester. And like you said, Jack and I can come over for a nice holiday in America.'

Helen heard the music from a long way off, coming from the direction of the ballroom of the Seattle hotel where they were staying. It was the last night of the conference.

The music from the Cajun band was unmistakable, toe-tappingly hypnotic…and it drew her towards it like a magnet.

'We've *got* to find out where that's coming from!' she said, dashing along the hotel corridor, following the sound as if it were being played by the Pied Piper.

Andrew had to break into a run to keep up with

her. As the sound got louder, Helen's enthusiasm
soared. They rounded a corner and found themselves
in the midst of a throng of people dancing to the
distinctive sounds of the Cajun band at the far end of
the large ballroom.

'This is my all-time favourite kind of music!' she
said, shouting to make herself heard.

Andrew took her hand and led her across the dance
floor, finding a small space amid the mass of gyrating
couples. He held her close, placing her arms round
his neck, and they began to dance slowly and sensually.

Her body seemed to melt into his in unspoken sur-
render. They remained tightly entwined in each
other's arms, dancing slowly and languidly—even
when the band switched to a faster rhythm. Filled
with desire and longing for him, Helen clung to him
tightly, never wanting the dance to end, never wanting
to let him go. She sensed he felt the same, the way
he ran his hands down her back, pressing her to him
as he moved against her in a manner that was unmis-
takably sexual.

It felt so good, so right...their bodies melting together as one. They couldn't be any closer—apart
from actually making love.

She moved her hands to the back of his head, entwining her fingers in his thick, dark hair. Andrew's
mouth found hers and he kissed her roughly, passionately and with a domination he'd not used before.
This time his kiss was different, hot and erotic, plun-
dering her mouth with a sweet invasion, his arousal
obvious to her in more ways than one.

By the time the band had struck up the first chords

of their next number, Helen and Andrew had left the ballroom and, wordlessly, were hurrying along the corridor to the hotel lift. They were the only people in it and almost missed their floor because they were kissing each other so ardently, completely oblivious to their surroundings.

Once inside his hotel room, Andrew shut the door firmly but not before placing the DO NOT DISTURB sign on the doorhandle. Leaning against the closed door, he pulled her roughly to him, kissing her hungrily, at the same time sliding his hand down the back of her dress, opening the zip fastener with one swift movement. Helen was equally impatient to remove Andrew's clothes and within moments of stepping into the room they each stood naked, surrounded by hastily discarded items of clothing.

Her heart was beating like a wild thing as he led her to the bed. Lying next to her, he gave a low moan as he ran his hands over her body. The look of desire on his face filled her with elation as his gaze covered every inch of her. Her mother had been right. Now she was sure that Andrew had been waiting for 'that special woman' and she was equally sure that she was the one. Surely only a special person could inspire such a look of ardour on a man's face?

They made love with an intensity she hadn't known she was capable of. They were like two untamed creatures ferocious with need for each other, abandoning themselves to reckless passion.

'Oh, God,' he said when it was over, his voice low and unsteady.

As he spoke it suddenly struck Helen that these were the first words either of them had uttered since they'd left the dance floor. She snuggled against him, sighing contentedly. She was truly delighted to discover that a man who, in his professional life, was so cool and clinical could also be so passionately sensual. She drifted off to sleep in his arms.

Andrew, however, was unable to sleep. The moment after they'd made love, he regretted it. Not the actual love-making, of course. That had been wonderful. *She* was wonderful. And that was the problem. He had wanted her so much...the way their bodies had become as one... Everything about her cried out to him to take her in his arms and love her again.

A great wave of guilt engulfed him, blotting out the sexual stirrings within his body. How *could* he have involved her in his life when he had nothing to offer her but uncertainty? How could he ask her to possibly sacrifice her own career for his? She was so trusting but she just didn't know what she'd be letting herself in for by getting involved with him. She could be putting at risk everything she'd worked for.

When he'd suggested they attend the Seattle conference he'd known there had been the possibility that they might end up in bed together. There was such a powerful attraction and sexual magnetism between them and for that reason he'd deliberately kept his distance. It had been that damned Cajun band and their hypnotic music that had drawn Helen onto the dance floor and into his arms. The moment their bodies had touched, her arms entwined around him and the sweet scent of her invading his senses, he'd known he was lost. All his good intentions had been thrown to the wind.

Andrew pressed his face into Helen's hair as the

conflicting emotions of guilt and desire battled on inside him. She stirred slightly but didn't wake. He
longed to run his hands over her drowsy body and
awaken her with kisses on her face, her breasts and
down across her hips and stomach as a prelude to
making love to her again, this time more slowly and
sensually in contrast to the urgent desperation of the
first time. But instead he sighed deeply and, turning
his back to her, tried to go to sleep.

Early next morning, Helen woke up and, stretching
and yawning, remembered where she was—and with
whom she had spent the night. A warm glow filled
her body. She turned over towards Andrew and snuggled up to him.

'Mmm,' she said, 'you smell good…all warm and
masculine and very desirable.' She ran her hand over
his body and down past the curve of his hip. He reacted like a scalded cat, swiftly moving away from
her probing hand and sitting up in the bed.

'What's the matter?' she asked huskily, amused at
first by his reaction.

He pulled away from her, swinging his legs over
the side of the bed, his back to her.

'I'm sorry about last night,' he said hoarsely. 'I
didn't mean for us to get involved like this.'

She looked at him, puzzled for a minute. 'What do
you mean?' She frowned.

The look on Helen's face, not surprisingly, was one
of hurt disbelief which only served to make Andrew
feel even more guilty.

He stood up and went into the bathroom, returning
almost immediately wearing a bathrobe.

'Let's just say the time isn't right for us,' he said, trying to soften the blow.

Helen pulled up the cotton sheet, covering her nakedness. She shivered involuntarily, shocked by Andrew's sudden and unexpected reaction.

'Why? What do you mean, Andrew?' she asked slowly, looking at him with eyes wide with shock, an empty feeling filling the pit of her stomach. 'I thought we had a good relationship.'

'We *have* a very good relationship,' he said carefully. 'A good *working* relationship.'

Shock suddenly turned to anger, the adrenalin of fury making her blood boil. 'That's not what I meant and you know it!' She looked at him scornfully. 'Frightened of any commitment, I suppose?'

He sat on the edge of the bed next to her and attempted to put a consoling arm around her shoulders. She shrugged it off.

'Helen, there's something I have to sort out, something to do with business—and I can only do it by myself. I don't want to get you involved. I have to go away shortly and I may be away for some time. So you see—'

'You sound like Captain Oates! Do me a favour, cut the heroics!'

Helen dragged the sheet off the bed and wrapped herself in it as she walked over to where her clothes were lying in a heap on the floor. She tried to keep her voice calm and level. 'That's the most feeble excuse I've heard in a long time for telling a woman you just want a one-night stand, no strings attached!'

'It's not like that,' he protested. 'Believe me, Helen.'

'Believe you? Why should I believe you? You're just a man who's scared of commitment, that's what you are!'

She grabbed her clothes and her handbag and, still with the sheet wrapped around her, opened the door. She was fuming, experiencing a furious mixture of emotions—a most unpleasant combination of anger, sorrow and humiliation.

'Oh, by the way,' she snapped at him. 'Where are you going away to for this thing you have to do by yourself?'

He hesitated for a beat before replying, 'Chicago.'

'Chicago! At least I know where that is. They call it the Windy City, don't they? How very appropriate! And when are you going?'

'In a few weeks' time,' he answered, looking and feeling wretched.

'I'll say goodbye now, then!' she threw back at him.

She stepped outside into the corridor, which was mercifully empty at that particular moment, slamming the door behind her. Her own hotel room was five doors away and she made the distance, wrapped in the bed sheet, unnoticed by any of the other hotel guests. She was in such a pent-up mood she wouldn't have given a damn if her outlandish exit from Andrew's room had been witnessed by a conference of church leaders.

Once inside her own room she stepped into the shower. She tried to blot out the memory of their delirious love-making of only a few short hours ago.

'That's something I must put right out of my mind,' she muttered to herself as the warm water washed off

the foaming shower gel. 'And something else…
somebody else I must put right out of my mind is
Andrew Henderson. I wish to heaven I'd never set
eyes on him.'

Another man Helen was beginning to wish she'd
never set eyes on was Professor Mulberry. Almost
from her first day at the Institute she'd been aware
that the director of sports science was taking more
than just a fatherly interest in her.

At least once a day he would call in at the laboratory on some pretext or other and make straight for
wherever Helen was standing or sitting. Mulberry was
one of those people, she decided, who seemed to in-
vade one's personal space. Whether or not it was de-
liberate, she was never too sure. She found it quite
unnerving as she inched away from him, only to realise that he was moving closer to her, inch-by-inch,
until invariably she ended up trapped in a corner or
against a bank of computers.

He would never actually touch her. No doubt he
was all too aware of the sexual harassment cases that
were detailed in all the newspapers. Nevertheless, she
found his interest in her creepy, particularly the way
his eyes would stray to her breasts or, if she was
seated, peer down her cleavage if she ever made the
mistake of opening more than a couple of buttons on
her blouse. He even asked her out on a date, having
made it crystal clear that he and Mrs Mulberry enjoyed the freedom of an 'open' marriage.

Helen turned him down as tactfully as she could
but found the experience very uncomfortable. She
told Marcie about it.

'We all know that Old Mulberry has the hots for you. We can see the way he drools over you—he can hardly keep his fat little paws off you!'

'At first I imagined he was just trying to be kind,' said Helen.

Marcie gave one of her high-pitched squawks. 'He's trying all right! And I've a good idea what he's trying for!'

Ten days after the Seattle conference Professor Mulberry called her into his office.

'I believe you were at a sports conference on the West Coast a couple of weeks back,' he said, not looking at all pleased.

'That's right, Professor. It was over a weekend and therefore I didn't take any time from my research at the Institute.'

'That's as may be,' he said putting his plump hands together in an attitude of prayer. He moved them to his equally plump lips as if to kiss them. He looked deep in thought. Helen remained silent wondering what, if anything, she'd done wrong.

'That's as may be,' he repeated. 'I believe, Dr Blackburn, you were in the company of Dr Henderson. Is that not so?'

On hearing Andrew's name mentioned, Helen blushed. For ten days she'd been trying to forget the damned man and she didn't want the professor reminding her about him.

'We were both at the conference, yes.' What was Mulberry getting at? Helen wondered.

'It has come to my notice that you and Dr Henderson are possibly becoming…how shall I put it? Becoming close. Would you say that was the case?'

Helen was irritated that Mulberry was asking her about her relationship with Andrew. It was really none of his business, but instead of rising to the bait she took a deep breath and replied calmly.

'Dr Henderson and I are not close. Not in the way you mean.'

Mulberry's facial expression relaxed. 'Ah,' he said. 'I'm glad to hear that, my dear. You see, I wouldn't want you to become too *embroiled* with him, if you follow my meaning.'

'Whatever are you talking about?'

'If you're not involved with him, there's nothing to concern yourself about. It's just that Dr Henderson has his own agenda, his own way of doing things, and I wouldn't want you getting caught up in…' He waved his hands in the air in his search for the correct word or phrase. It escaped him so he left the sentence unfinished.

Helen narrowed her eyes.

'What are you telling me about Dr Henderson?'

Mulberry put on an innocent, wide-eyed look. 'Nothing. Nothing specific. You see, I feel a certain responsibility for you, my dear, having brought you over here. I wouldn't want you getting…*embroiled* in anything.'

Embroiled… He'd said that before. It was a word that could mean anything and Helen was no nearer to knowing what Mulberry was on about.

As she rose to leave, he leaned over the desk and said conspiratorially, 'You know about Chicago?'

'He told me he had to go there for some time to sort something out.'

'Well, there you are,' said Mulberry, moving from his desk to the door. He tapped an index finger against the side of his nose. 'The least said the better.'

He was, as usual, standing very close to her and she had to brush against him to get through the door. He put out a hand as she passed him and it touched her on the breast. He pretended it was an accident.

'Sorry, my dear. I was just about to say I have tickets for *Swan Lake* at the Lincoln Centre. A wonderful performance, by all accounts. I wondered if by chance you might like to accompany me on Friday evening?'

The combination of Mulberry touching her and at the same time hitting on her for a date made Helen feel nauseous.

'I'm afraid I can't,' she said quickly. 'I'm going out with Jane, my flatmate.'

She walked swiftly away in case Mulberry had been about to say he'd change the tickets for another day.

Following the Seattle weekend, Andrew tried on several occasions to get in touch with Helen by telephone, but she didn't return his calls. When he attempted to see her in the Institute, she just froze him out and walked away without letting him speak to her. In July, a few weeks later, Jane thought she had some news for her flatmate.

'He's gone to Chicago!' she announced as she let herself into the apartment one evening after work. 'Your gorgeous Dr Henderson…off to Chicago, just like that! We're all heartbroken in the ER because, as you know, we all fancy him like mad—'

'I know,' interrupted Helen, continuing to stir-fry the freshly chopped vegetables.

'You know that we all fancy him like mad? Yes, I know that you know that—because I'm always telling you so!' Jane flopped down on the kitchen chair in an exaggerated gesture of exhaustion.

'I know about Chicago,' said Helen. 'He told me he was going.' She carried on with the cooking, not daring to let Jane see the distressed look on her face. Even though she'd known Andrew was leaving New York she hadn't been sure exactly when that would be. Jane had now confirmed he'd gone...and it all seemed so final.

'You knew?' Jane was flabbergasted. 'You knew he was going to Chicago and yet you never said anything?'

'Why should I?' Helen put on a bright smile. 'I'd got lots of other things on my mind...getting on with my research and looking for a job for when the funding ends...'

'But I thought you were very keen on the gorgeous Andrew? He leaves enough messages for you on our answering-machine...I imagined there was a hot romance going on...'

'Well, there isn't! Now, can we please change the subject? What flavour of stir-fry sauce do you want with this?' She picked up two small jars and read the labels. 'Black bean or sweet and sour?'

'Sweet and sour,' said Jane. 'It reminds me of you and Andrew. First it was all sweet and now it seems to have gone sour! Hey!' She ducked just in time to miss being struck by the oven glove thrown by Helen.

Two weeks later, Helen was on her own walking down Fifth Avenue, enjoying the bustling atmosphere and looking up from time to time at the patches of blue sky that were visible between the towering buildings.

She'd picked up a couple of good book bargains and was now heading for the area near Rockefeller Center and the Lower Plaza which in summer was turned into a sunken restaurant. She joined the tourists and sightseers leaning over the rails taking in the scene below. In the winter, Andrew told her, it was made into an ice rink. He'd promised her that if she was still in New York he'd take her there to skate on New Year's Eve. Well, if she took this job she'd been offered she'd still be able to go skating there—never mind needing him to take her!

Clutching her books to her body, she had a moment's light-headedness and thought she might fall over. It was the daydreaming that was playing tricks on her. She still hadn't got Andrew out of her mind and part of her was beginning to weaken. *If* he came back from Chicago in a few months' time, and *if* he appeared more ready for commitment, maybe they would be skating together on Rockefeller Plaza on New Year's Eve after all.

She was startled from her reverie by a woman's voice saying, 'Is it you? Excuse me, but aren't you the friend of Dr Henderson?'

She turned sharply to her right and saw a woman who looked vaguely familiar.

'I do know Dr Henderson,' Helen replied, adding anxiously, 'Has anything happened to him? I'm sorry…I just can't recall who you are.'

'Oh, pardon me,' said the woman. 'I'm Mary Oberon. You and Dr Henderson very kindly came to my aid when I broke my wrist playing tennis a while back. My husband, Tim Oberon, is a lawyer and he knows your friend Dr Henderson professionally.'

Helen instantly remembered the woman and the unusual circumstances of her injury. She looked down at Mary's wrist and saw it was strapped with bandaging.

'The lady with suspected osteoporosis?'

'That's the one!' She lifted her right arm slightly, holding it steady with her left hand. 'Your diagnosis was correct, I'm afraid to say. So, no more tennis for me…and I'm on a regime of bone-strengthening medication, special diet and only very gentle exercise.'

'I'm sorry to hear that,' said Helen sympathetically. 'It's a wretched condition and you're very young to be affected.'

'I'll live with it!' said Mary cheerfully. 'I've got used to it now and I'm very glad of the warning. At least I can try and do something about it—hormones and all that stuff. The silly thing is, I was only playing tennis to keep my husband company. I don't care too much for the game myself. I just didn't want him playing tennis with all those glamorous young women in skimpy tennis dresses…but I guess I'll just have to trust him.'

Mary laughed merrily but it sounded more like bravado to Helen. She joined in the laughter.

'Dr Henderson is away in Chicago, so I hear,' said

Mary. 'Tim mentioned it the other day. His law firm is connected to the Chicago law firm Dr Henderson is dealing with.'

This was news to Helen. Why on earth was Andrew 'dealing with' a law firm in Chicago?

'So,' Helen said lightly, 'your husband's a lawyer? I think I remember Dr Henderson mentioning something about that. What kind of work does he specialise in?'

'Divorce,' said Mary. 'He's one of the best, though I say it myself. Actually…' she leaned nearer to Helen '…that's how we met. A partner of his was handling my divorce from my first husband. Anyway, it's lovely seeing you again, Dr?'

'Blackburn,' said Helen, trying to hide the shock she'd experienced on being told that Andrew was somehow involved with lawyers in Chicago, lawyers who specialised in divorce.

'The plot thickens,' said Jane when Helen told her of the conversation she'd had with Mary Oberon three days previously. Jane had been home to stay with her folks for the weekend and this was the first opportunity Helen had had to tell her the latest twist in the Andrew saga.

'The word around the hospital,' said Jane, 'is that he had to go to Chicago for his career. He used to work there and we all imagined he'd been head-hunted and was made an offer he couldn't refuse.'

The two girls were drinking ice-cold canned cola, with the air-conditioning on full and the windows tightly shut against the sticky heat of the humid August day.

'Maybe he made up the career thing,' said Helen. 'Perhaps it was all a big excuse to hide the fact that he was getting a divorce.'

'Why should he do that? There's no shame in being divorced or getting divorced. Not in America... certainly not in New York.'

'But that would make him out to be a liar,' said Helen. 'On our very first date I asked him if he was married or anything—meaning going steady, engaged or divorced or whatever—and he said, quite categorically, no. His exact words were "not even anything".'

'So, what else could it be?' Jane pondered the puzzle.

'I bet there's a woman in there somewhere,' said Helen bitterly. 'The way he was terrified of getting involved with anyone else...as if that might be held against him.'

Jane sat up on the settee as if struck by another idea. 'Could it be that *he* isn't getting divorced, but that *she* is?'

'Who?'

'This other woman. The one he went back to Chicago for?'

The two women sat in silence as they worked out this new scenario.

'You could be right, Jane. That would explain a lot. So, he's fallen in love with this married woman who won't leave her husband. Andrew moves to New York, hoping to forget about her. Then the woman decides she wants Andrew and will get a divorce after all.'

'The bastard!' said Jane, clutching Helen on the

arm. 'I know you loved him. You didn't have to tell me that. And I know you're trying to get over him, so I won't mention his name ever again.'

They sat in companionable silence, each pretending not to notice the large tear that was trickling down Helen's cheek.

'I've got something to tell you,' Helen said.

Jane looked at her expectantly.

'I'm not staying on in New York after my research funding finishes. I'm not going to accept that job in sports medicine.'

'Oh, Helen!' Jane was surprised and upset by this revelation.

'It won't affect you because it'll be after you've moved to the hospital in your home town…'

'I was thinking of you, not me,' said Jane. 'You were so looking forward to staying on in New York, even without Andrew. That's what you said. To hell with him, you said.'

Helen was silent for a what seemed an age, trying to find the right words.

'I've got something else to tell you.' She stood up and walked to the picture window with its dramatic view. 'I'm pregnant.'

CHAPTER FIVE

'PREGNANT?' Jane sounded incredulous. 'How did that happen?'

Helen gave a hollow laugh. 'Oh, the usual way.'

'Well, I guessed as much as that! But you had me fooled...I didn't know you and Andrew were, you know?' Jane paused. 'It *is* Andrew's baby, I presume? I mean, you're not having a secret affair with someone else?'

'Of course not!' retorted Helen. 'And, yes, it is Andrew's baby. It happened in Seattle. What I thought was going to be the start of a wonderful love affair turned out—for him—to be a one-night stand.' Helen paused for a moment. 'And before you ask, yes, we did use contraception!'

'Must have failed, huh?' said Jane, stating the obvious.

Helen shrugged. 'I guess so.' Her lip began to tremble.

'Oh, honey, you poor lamb!' Jane hugged her friend. After a few moments she said. 'You were in Seattle in June, right?'

Helen nodded.

'Nearly two months ago?'

She nodded again.

'So it's early days. You can still decide to...have it...or not to have it.'

Helen wiped away a couple of tears that had trickled down her cheeks. 'I've been wrestling with that thought for the past month, ever since the day I missed my first period.'

'You knew you were pregnant and you kept it to yourself?'

'I didn't know definitely,' replied Helen. 'I had my suspicions but I didn't do the pregnancy test until this weekend. Somehow I couldn't bring myself to face the reality of it until I'd come to a decision about my future with Andrew. I thought I might tell him, even though he was going to Chicago, but after meeting Mary Oberon and discovering that he's involved with divorce lawyers I realised that there was no future for us after all.'

'Are you going to have an abortion? No one would blame you if you did.'

Helen stiffened. 'I couldn't do it, Jane. I know I could never live with myself afterwards. When I saw the positive window show up on the test kit, all at once the baby became a reality. My baby…Andrew's baby. You're right, Jane, I did love him so much…and I know I could never get rid of any baby, let alone *his* baby. I expect you think I'm a silly sentimental fool.' She wiped away more tears.

Jane hugged her tightly. 'I don't think you're silly at all,' she said. 'I'd probably do the same thing myself.'

The two girls said nothing for a while, taking comfort from each other. Then Jane spoke.

'Are you going to tell Andrew? Even if he's involved with another woman, don't you think he has the right to know he's going to be a father?'

Helen pondered the question.

'I'll tell him one day,' she said. 'One day when I've got my own life in order and I can cope with his reaction.'

Jane was dubious. 'Don't you think you should tell him now, before the baby's born? It might make a difference to how he views his present relationship.'

Helen looked down at her feet before facing her friend. 'Well, he gave his phone number in Chicago in one of his messages on our answering-machine and actually I have tried phoning him on several occasions.'

'And?'

'I can never get through to him. I don't want to leave a message on his answering-machine saying "I'm pregnant", do I? And yesterday a woman answered his phone and gave me the distinct impression that she was intercepting his calls.'

Jane's eyes widened. 'Intercepting his calls? You mean, like finding out who's calling and then saying he's not in?'

'Exactly.'

'Do you think it was her? This divorcee woman?'

Helen shrugged again. 'Who knows? So that seems to be the end of that, and it's back home for me.'

Jane's face dropped. 'You don't need to go home, honey. You can still work over here. What about that terrific job you were offered?'

Helen shook her head. 'It's no good, Jane. In order to be able to cope on my own with a baby I need to go back to Milchester where I've got all the back-up support from my family.'

Jane agreed reluctantly. 'What did your mom say when you told her?'

Helen shifted uneasily on the couch.

'I haven't told her yet.'

Jane breathed in sharply, then gave a low whistle. 'When will you?'

Helen considered it for a while then, checking her watch to work out the time difference, said, 'I suppose there's no time like the present.'

Helen's mother, although she must have been shocked rigid by her daughter's news, appeared calm and comforting at the other end of the phone.

'Of course you must come home,' she said. 'We'll always be here for you, Helen, you know that. And how exciting it will be to have a grandchild in the house. All our friends have grandchildren…we were beginning to feel left out.'

'I won't be a burden on you, Mum,' Helen said, desperate to reassure her mother. 'I'll get work as a locum. There are bound to be lots of that kind of job going, and after the baby's born I'll pick up locum work again for a while until I can get my sports medicine career back on the road.'

She made her voice sound positive and upbeat, trying to convince herself as much as anyone else that this accidental baby wasn't going to make any difference to her career plans. But both she and her mother knew that she was bluffing. Andrew's baby was going to change her life—and her career prospects—and although she instinctively knew that she would love the baby with her whole heart, she also knew it heralded the end of this particular phase of her life.

*   *   *

The professor called Helen into his room a few days later.

'I was wondering what your plans were for the future,' he said. 'The Moreton funding runs out at the end of this month, as you know, but I sincerely hope that we won't be losing you back to the old country.' He laughed as he used what he imagined to be a quaint turn of phrase. 'You have done some remarkable research in the six months you've been here and I think you can still teach us "old colonials" a thing or two over here in the New World.' He chuckled again at his *bon mot*.

'I'm afraid I *will* be going back home, Professor,' said Helen not daring to make eye contact with him.

'But I'd heard on the grapevine that you'd been offered a job in sports medicine in New York. In my opinion that would appear to be the best move you could make at this point in your career.'

'I was offered a job, but have decided to go back to England,' said Helen. 'Homesick, you know.'

'Homesick for a young man, perhaps?' enquired the professor.

Helen smiled politely, giving nothing away.

Helen was all packed up and ready to leave for the airport. She and Jane had said their farewells, exchanging addresses and promising to keep in touch.

Her flatmate was herself leaving New York the following month, returning to Iowa to take up a job in a large hospital near her home town. Looking at the note she'd been handed by Helen, she checked the details. 'Your name is Blackburn, and your mother's name is Talbot, right?'

'That's my stepfather's name. I chose to keep my real father's name.'

'Now, you *will* let me know about the baby, won't you?' Jane's lower lip began to tremble. 'I feel so bad, not being around to help you through all this.'

'It's my decision,' said Helen. 'I'm a big girl and I know exactly what I'm getting myself into, so don't be feeling sorry for me. And remember your promise?'

'Promise?'

'That you'll be the godmother.'

'You bet!' enthused Jane. 'And if I can't get over in person we can do it by... What's that thing called—poxy?'

Helen giggled. 'I think you mean proxy.'

'Knew it was something that sounded like a disease! On second thoughts I'll get myself over there!'

Helen had been back in England a month when Andrew turned up at her apartment in New York. Now that the Chicago business was behind him, he was desperately keen to make contact with Helen again. He wished he'd been able to confide in her at the time, but he was convinced it would have been totally irresponsible of him to involve her in his problems.

He rang the buzzer and a man answered the intercom.

'There's no one here called Helen,' said the disembodied voice. 'We've just moved in. Maybe she was the previous occupant.'

'What about her room-mate, Jane? Is she there?' Andrew asked.

'No. It's just guys in here now. No girls, I'm sorry to say.'

Andrew could hear a throaty male laugh over the intercom before it went dead.

'Damn,' he said, turning on his heel and hailing a cab.

Andrew found Professor Mulberry in his office at the Institute.

'Dr Blackburn has finished her research at the Institute,' he was told. 'I'm surprised to learn that she did not keep you informed of her whereabouts.'

Pompous ass, thought Andrew, itching to respond with a cutting comment. He decided, however, that he'd better keep calm and not antagonise the wretched man.

'Do you have a contact address you could let me have for her, please?' he requested politely.

For at least a minute the professor remained silent, folding his hands together and adopting a far-away look.

'I don't think that would be appropriate, do you, Dr Henderson?'

'Sorry? What do you mean, appropriate? I'm asking for the address of a medical colleague, not—' He'd been about to add 'not explicit nude photographs', but he checked himself just in time.

'I'm sure that if Dr Blackburn had wished you to have her forwarding address she would have given it to you herself.' He fixed the younger man with an innocent stare.

He's enjoying this, thought Andrew. Helen had told him of the fixation the professor had for her and how she'd always had to escape his unwanted attentions.

Mulberry was jealous of the obvious attraction Andrew and Helen had for each other and he was going to make him pay for it.

'You could interpret it that way, Professor,' said Andrew coolly. 'But because I had to go to Chicago at short notice our lines must have got crossed…and, well, to be perfectly frank I thought she was still in New York. It never occurred to me that she might have gone… Where did you say she'd gone?'

'I don't recall saying where she'd gone.'

Hell! The man was infuriating!

'I got a message that she'd tried to contact me in Chicago. It was most unfortunate that she wasn't put through to me at the time.'

'Indeed,' said Mulberry with a smile.

Andrew waited for a moment, hoping the professor would relent. But instead he just smiled superciliously at him.

'So you're not prepared to give me the address?' said Andrew.

Mulberry took his time before replying.

'It would appear that way, Dr Henderson. You see, there may well be someone else involved. A boy-friend. She implied as much to me. As your William Shakespeare said, ''Discretion is the better part of valour.'' He tapped the side of his nose with his index finger, hugely enjoying his position of power. The lovely Helen may have spurned his own advances but he was darned if he was going to let her fall into the hands of this confidently handsome Brit. He'd have to do a good deal more grovelling before he'd get any joy out of Alan J. Mulberry.

*   *   *

Helen had been back in Milchester for less than two weeks before she found herself a locum job. It was in the city centre, at Milchester General, as a doctor in the orthopaedic outpatients department. Her mother worked part time at the same hospital as a nurse.

The locum job suited Helen very well, keeping her extremely busy and giving her no time at all to brood about what she'd left behind in New York...and about who she'd left behind in Chicago.

A few months later she met a man called Patrick. He was a doctor from a local medical centre and had referred an orthopaedic patient to her. He was recently divorced and they each recognised in the other their own vulnerability and hurt.

They went out together a few times.

'He's a very sweet guy,' Helen told her mother, 'and it's nice to have someone to go to the cinema, or have a drink with. But, of course, we're only friends. Good friends.'

Her mother winked at her. 'You might become *very good* friends one day.'

Helen laughed. 'It's not like that, Mum. Patrick and I could never be an item because for a start I don't find him sexy. And he's not going to be interested in me in that kind of way because I'm not a redhead.'

'Pardon? Did you say redhead?'

Helen laughed, seeing her mother's puzzled expression. 'Patrick tells me he's always been mad on redheads. His first wife had flaming tresses and he always raves about women with similar looks.'

'Oh, dear,' said her mother in disappointment.

'But don't you see? That's the beauty of it!' said Helen. 'We each feel quite safe emotionally. I know he's not going to get keen on me, not with my dark hair. And he knows I'm not going to start demanding commitment from him. He says it really is like having the best of both worlds.'

Helen patted her expanding bump. 'He loves taking a personal interest in my pregnancy, knowing at the same time that he's not going to have to support us both when the time comes! The great thing about Patrick and me is that we're just good friends and you can never have too many of those.'

CHAPTER SIX

'THAT is the most gorgeous baby boy I've ever seen,' said the Irish midwife, handing the baby to Helen.

It had been a long, hard labour and, quite frankly, by the end of it she couldn't have cared less whether the baby was gorgeous or not…just as long as the torment was over and the child was healthy.

Helen's mother had been with her during the long hours of labour, and Patrick had called in at the labour ward at the crucial time and had also been able to give Helen moral as well as practical support.

'I never want to have another baby in my life!' she said, cradling the tiny, screwed-up scrap of humanity in her arms.

'Ah, sure, that's what they all say,' said the midwife. 'And you know what I say to them? See you in two years' time!'

'Well done, Helen,' said Patrick, stroking the baby's shock of dark hair. 'He's a great little chap. What are you going to call him?'

'Robert,' she said without hesitation. 'It was my father's name.' Then, looking across at her mother, she said, 'I think Daddy would have liked that, don't you?'

'Yes, darling,' said her mother, becoming misty-eyed. 'He'd have liked that very much.'

When the baby was two months old, Helen and her mother discussed arrangements for the christening.

'June would be nice,' said her mother. 'The garden will be looking its best, and we can have champagne and strawberries on the lawn and—'

'What if it rains?' said her stepfather, always a practical man.

'It wouldn't dare! But if it did, we can have it inside and just look out onto the garden. Either way, that's the best time to have it. Also,' added her mother, 'if we wait much longer, little Robert won't fit into the family christening robe.'

'That sounds fine to me,' agreed Helen. 'I'll have to check with Jane to see what date suits her best. I really want her to come over and be the godmother. And it will be great to see her again.'

'Who's going to be the godfather?' enquired her mother.

'I asked Patrick,' said Helen. 'He's been so good to me and he loves little Robert.'

'I think he's pretty keen on you, too,' said her stepfather, smiling knowingly. 'He'd make a very good husband and father, you know.'

'Jack!' said her mother crossly. 'It's none of our business. Don't start saying embarrassing things like that, and certainly don't be saying it at the christening!'

'I speak with authority on the subject,' persisted Jack. 'After all, I am a stepfather, and there's no reason why this Patrick shouldn't be one as well!'

Her mother shot an exasperated look at her husband, but Helen just laughed.

'Don't let him tease you, Mum. Jack knows as well as I do that there's a lot more to being a stepfather than he implies. For a start, you were in love with each other. I'm not in love with Patrick, and he's not in love with me…and he never will be.'

'Why not?' asked Jack.

'Because I haven't got red hair, that's why not!'

Jack, unwilling to admit defeat, said, 'You could always dye it!'

Even so, Helen and Patrick became very close, drawn to each other because of their shared love of baby Robert. Patrick would often spend his evenings at her house and she found his company relaxing and comforting.

It was becoming obvious to Helen that Patrick was not only keen on the baby, he was getting very keen on her, too. At first she wondered if she should warn him off, tell him that she could never really love him because she was still madly in love with Andrew. But then she began to take a more realistic view of life. She would never meet anyone like Andrew again. Was she going to spend the rest of her life regretting that she'd ever set eyes on him, regretting that her baby would grow up without a father? Or should she settle for a good, caring man like Patrick?

One evening she had a conversation with her mother that made her realise she had to make a decision about her future—and the sooner the better.

'I've got something to tell you,' said her mother as she was doing the ironing in the kitchen.

Helen could sense that her mother had something on her mind—something that she was finding a little embarrassing or awkward.

'Is anything the matter, Mum?'

'No, not really,' she said, concentrating hard on the ironing, not meeting Helen's gaze. 'It's just that Jack has decided he's going to retire at the end of the year. He's sixty-three and we thought it would be nice to have some time together, travelling around, before we get too decrepit!'

'Decrepit! You're ten years younger than Jack… and he's fit as a butcher's dog! It'll be a long time before you two turn into wrinklies!'

'So you won't mind?' her mother asked anxiously.

'I don't mind Jack retiring. Why should I?'

'Well, that's just it,' said her mother, putting the iron down on its stand. 'It might affect you. You and Robert. So that's why I told Jack I had to discuss it with you and that we wouldn't do anything unless you agreed.'

'What is there to discuss…to agree?'

'We'd always talked about what we'd do when Jack retired. I would take early retirement from the hospital and we'd buy one of those mobile homes, camper van things, and drive all over Europe, spending months away at a time. Jack would like us to take up skiing again and spend, say, a month in a French or Austrian ski resort. And then in the summer we've got a long list of countries we'd like to visit…and we'd be able to spend several weeks at a time without needing to come home after a fortnight.'

'Oh,' said Helen, suddenly seeing where this was leading.

'We also discussed selling this house and buying a smaller one. But I told Jack that we couldn't do that yet because we need all the rooms.'

'Because of me and Robert?' Helen was beginning to get the picture.

'Partly,' said her mother, meaning 'yes'.

'You mustn't let us stop you from doing what you'd always planned, Mum. That wouldn't be fair on you and Jack.'

'I knew you'd say that, love. You're such a kind, thoughtful girl. But I told Jack that we couldn't possibly put our plans into action—selling the house, buying a camper van and everything—until I knew how things were going to work out for you and little Robert. You see, darling, it would mean I wouldn't be around to have him while you were at work. I'd feel I was deserting you in your hour of need.'

'Oh, Mum, you've never done that! I don't know what I would have done without your help in recent months, but things are beginning to look up now. By the time Jack retires, I have a feeling that Robert and I will be taken care of.'

The next day, Patrick came to pick up Helen and Robert to take them on a day out to the seaside. As they were driving along the motorway she could sense that he, too, like her mother the previous evening, had something on his mind.

'Well, go on,' she said, 'spit it out!'

He laughed. 'Is it that obvious?'

'You haven't spoken a word since we stopped for coffee at that last service station,' said Helen, 'so you might as well tell me now if there's anything the matter. Is there?'

Patrick took a deep breath. 'No, there's nothing the matter,' he said. 'I was going to ask you something, that's all.'

She said nothing.

'Helen,' he said, after a long pause, 'why don't we get married?'

At that moment, Robert began squeaking and Helen turned to the back seat to pacify him. When he was settled, she turned back to Patrick.

'Are you sure?' she asked in return. 'Are you sure you really want to marry me, or do you just love Robert? Because you can always be special to him…'

'I'm asking you to marry me,' said Patrick. 'I love you, Helen.'

'I thought you were mad on redheads!' She found herself joking because this was the first time Patrick had declared his love for her and she wasn't sure how she was going to take it. Up till now they had been good friends. He was now turning the relationship into something it had never been before. She needed a little breathing space to decide on her reply.

He sighed. 'Being mad on redheads was just me being superficial,' he said. 'That was probably my problem all along! In the past I've been totally ruled by my emotions in my preference for that kind of woman. It's quite irrational.'

'You may regret it,' she said. 'You may regret marrying me, because I'm still in love with Andrew. I couldn't accept your proposal unless you knew that. But, as you also know, there's no chance Andrew will ever be a part of my life again…'

'I realise that, and I'm not expecting miracles,' said Patrick. 'I know all about Andrew—you've never held back any secrets from me. But I love baby Robert, and you must admit that it would be so much better for him to be brought up by two parents. I know I could provide a good home for all of us.'

Helen felt tears pricking her eyes. 'You're a very kind man, Patrick.'

'I'm very practical,' he said. 'I've worked it all out. We could pay for a baby-minder for when you're working…you could find a new job in sports medicine, like you said you wanted to, with more convenient hours. I have my own house and a reasonable amount of savings—even after paying off my ex-wife! You may not love me the way I love you, but I hope at least that you're fond of me.'

'Oh, yes,' said Helen quickly. 'I really *am* fond of you. And I would love to marry you, Patrick.' She put her hand over his and gave it a gentle squeeze.

He grinned. He looked so happy it almost made her believe that she was going to be as happy married to him as she would have been if she'd married Andrew. She found herself grinning as well. It was all going to work out fine. She would make Patrick happy, and the baby would have a doting father, and her parents could retire and drive away into the sunset in their camper van. It sounded a pretty good compromise to her.

When Helen told Dorothy the news, her mother's jaw dropped in amazement, and then her whole face lit up with a beaming smile. 'Oh, Helen! That's such good news!'

She hugged her daughter, jostling the feeding bottle. Robert clung to the teat for dear life, sucking away vigorously.

'Patrick is such a nice man. Jack and I think so, anyway. He'll make a wonderful father for little Robert.'

'That's what I thought,' said Helen.

'And, of course, he'll make a good husband, too,' she added hastily. 'I'm sure he'll want to prove he can make this marriage work. He's made mistakes in the past and has the divorce to show for it…but we mustn't hold that against him.'

'I wouldn't dream of holding that against him,' said Helen. 'After all, he's not the only one who's made mistakes.'

Shortly before Helen was due to return to work after her maternity leave, her mother came home from the hospital with some disturbing news.

'I've heard there's a new consultant at Milchester General,' she said. 'An orthopaedic surgeon.'

'Oh, really?' said Helen, not particularly interested. She was changing Robert's nappy and trying to put the clean one on while he wriggled like a slippery eel. Her mother stood in the doorway, not moving an inch.

Helen glanced quickly at her and back again to the squirming baby.

'Anything the matter, Mum?'

'I'm not sure,' said her mother. 'This new surgeon…his name is Dr Henderson.'

'Oh,' said Helen, a coldness striking her. She fixed the nappy on the baby and picked him up, holding him against her shoulder.

'I just thought I should tell you,' said her mother, her face tense.

'I'm sure it's just a coincidence,' said Helen, gently rocking the baby. 'Henderson isn't a particularly *un-usual* name, is it? I once had a dentist called John Henderson, I seem to remember.'

When Robert was three months old, Helen went back to work two full days and one morning a week as an orthopaedic locum at Milchester General in the hospital's new open access unit.

On her first day back she drove into the hospital car park in her mother's old red Metro, parking it in the area reserved for staff. She was told by one of the receptionists in the busy main hall of Milchester General that the open access unit was on the first floor of the building. She was just about to walk away when she noticed the list of consultants who had clinics that day. One of them was a Dr Henderson.

'This Dr Henderson,' she said to the receptionist, 'do you know what his first name is?'

She shook her head. 'He's new,' she said. 'Maybe Shirley knows.' She called across to her colleague. 'Shirley, do you know what Dr Henderson's name is?'

'Alastair, I think,' said Shirley.

Helen breathed a sigh of relief and was picking up her bag to walk to the stairs when Shirley corrected herself.

'No, it's not Alastair. It's something else beginning with A...Andrew, I think it is.'

Once the morning's work had begun, Helen didn't have too much time to dwell on the possibility that Andrew could be under the same roof. The whole idea was preposterous, she'd decided. For a start he was in Chicago, or at a pinch New York...certainly not Milchester!

'Who do we have next?' Helen asked the clinic nurse as she surveyed the waiting area which was now beginning to thin out.

'Mr Birdwell,' the nurse announced. Under her breath, she said to Helen, 'He's a traveller.'

'You mean he's on holiday here?'

'No,' she hissed. 'He's a gypsy...only we're not meant to call them that now. It's not politically correct!'

Mr Birdwell, an elderly, ruddy-faced man dressed in rough but not dirty clothes, followed the nurse into Helen's examination room. He was walking stiffly and leaning heavily on a stick.

'What can we do for you, Mr Birdwell?' asked Helen, after sitting him down on a chair facing her.

'It's my knee, Doctor. It's causing me terrible pain when I do the dancing.' Mr Birdwell spoke in an almost impenetrable Irish brogue.

'What kind of dancing?' asked Helen.

'Tap and clog,' he replied with pride. 'The hard-shoe dancing. Done it since I was a lad, but unfortunately I haven't been doing it regular. Not for quite a long time. Then at a shindig last night they called on me to do my stuff and, like a silly fool, I did. I think I must have twisted the old knee. Hurts like blazes, that's for sure.'

Helen and the nurse exchanged glances, keeping their faces straight. The idea of this game old gent doing the vigorous taps and knee-kicks of Irish dancing conjured up a delightful picture.

'If you'll go into the cubicle, Mr Birdwell, slip off your trousers and get onto the examination couch, I'll have a look at your knee,' instructed Helen, who was washing her hands in readiness.

Mr Birdwell's knee was swollen and Helen noticed some areas of bruising.

'Describe what action you were actually doing when you injured your knee,' Helen said.

'I was doing the hop and twist just before I swing my knee at right angles across the other leg. It's quite a tricky step and I was renowned for it. I could have taught these modern Irish dancers a thing or two in my day, I can tell you!'

Helen felt around the knee area and was convinced that this elderly man had suffered an injury more commonly seen in much younger athletes.

'I suspect you may have torn the ligament in your knee—the anterior cruciate ligament,' she explained to him. 'First of all we need to have an X-ray to rule out any fractures. Then we can take it from there. It may be that you'll need to be seen by someone in the orthopaedic department.'

She wrote his details on a form and gave it to him.

'The nurse will show you where the X-ray department is,' she said. 'When you've had it done, come back here and we can then decide on the best course of action.'

It was another hour before all the patients had been seen and by then Mr Birdwell had returned, holding his X-ray in a brown envelope.

'Shall I direct him to the orthopaedic department, Dr Blackburn?' the clinic nurse asked.

'Not yet,' she replied. 'I'll take a look at the X-ray first.'

She pinned the negative onto the light-box on the wall and studied it carefully.

'I can't see any bone fractures, which leads me to believe that my initial diagnosis was correct…a damaged ACL. In any event, the next stage is for Mr Birdwell to be assessed by an orthopaedic surgeon for possible arthroscopic surgery. First of all, though, we need to immobilise his knee in a leg brace to avoid further injury. And now that we've finished here, I might as well take him along to Orthopaedics myself and discuss Mr Birdwell's treatment with the consultant,' said Helen. 'If we can borrow a wheelchair, I can get him along there in no time. I'd feel happier knowing that his injury will be treated as soon as possible. It's important that the damaged tissue is repaired at an early stage. The longer it's left untreated, the longer it will take to cure, and the greater the chance of permanent disability.'

Helen could see the nurse looking at her with raised eyebrows.

'Sports injuries are my thing,' she said by way of explanation. 'I suppose you could count vigorous tap dancing as a type of sport!'

'Why don't I take Mr Birdwell?' suggested the nurse.

'It's OK. I've finished for the day and I may as well take this opportunity to have a word with the orthopaedic consultant. It would help if you rang on ahead to make sure they'll be expecting us.'

As Helen pushed Mr Birdwell along the hospital corridors she realised that she had a hidden agenda. All right, so it would be useful to speak directly to the consultant about the patient, but it was mainly to satisfy her curiosity about this new Dr Henderson. It couldn't possibly be *him*…could it?

It had been a hectic morning in Orthopaedics. Andrew was glad the clinic was almost over and he could look forward to relaxing for an hour before starting the afternoon surgery list.

It was only his second week in the job and he was only now settling into a proper routine, getting the feel of the place and, against all expectations, beginning to enjoy his new appointment. Being an orthopaedic consultant in Milchester was something he'd never thought he'd be. It just hadn't been in his career plan. But there again, so many things that had happened over the past year had also not been in his career plan. The months he'd been forced to spend in Chicago, for instance, and all the surrounding unpleasantness. Meeting Helen in New York and falling for her, just at the worst possible time, had also not been part of his overall strategy. And when he'd returned from Chicago, he'd expected to find her in New York—not back home in Milchester.

It had taken quite a bit of searching around for her, but he'd been pretty confident that she'd come back to her home town. That was why, when he'd seen this job advertised in a medical journal, he'd applied straight away. It was only for six months and that suited him fine. He'd been confident of tracking her down in that time and hopeful of convincing her that he really did love her, even though his past actions might have given the opposite impression.

Now that he was settled into the job, he decided that he'd start his search for her in earnest. He'd tried looking in the local phone book, without success. But then he recalled that Helen had a stepfather and therefore, if she was living at home, the phone number would be listed under a different name.

He was pondering what his next move should be—perhaps he should contact one of the professional organisations and try and get a lead from there—when he received a phone call from the open access clinic. Something about a patient with a suspect knee injury. He liked knees…they were his favourite thing, so to speak.

'Come this way,' he heard the desk nurse say to the patient. 'Dr Henderson is expecting you.'

An old man in a wheelchair was manoeuvred into his room. The wheelchair was being pushed by Helen Blackburn. Andrew beamed at her with delight. He could hardly believe his luck. Only a few days in Milchester and his search was over before it had hardly begun!

'Helen!' he exclaimed.

'Oh!' she blurted out. 'It *is* you!'

'So it would appear,' he said, attempting to keep his voice on an even keel.

What he instinctively wanted to do was to leap across the room and enfold her in his arms. She looked even lovelier than he remembered. Her thick, dark, shoulder-length hair had been cut shorter, but not too short. It suited her. But there was something else different about her, something…indefinable. She stared at him from sea-blue eyes, stared at him in…amazement? Delight? Horror? Whatever she felt at that precise moment, she was giving nothing away. After her initial reaction at seeing him, a shutter came down and she covered up her emotions. Her face became an inscrutable mask.

'You two know each other?' asked the nurse.

'We've met,' said Helen.

'In New York,' said Andrew.

'Oh, that's nice,' said the nurse, before going over to Mr Birdwell to collect his medical details.

Helen, her voice level and calm, gave her assessment of the patient's injuries and her initial diagnosis to Andrew. She hardly dared to look him in the eye. When she stopped speaking there was a moment's awkward pause.

'Dr Blackburn,' said Andrew, speaking in the same professional tone adopted by Helen, 'why don't we meet in the canteen for a coffee to catch up on old times?' He could see she was hesitating, possibly about to refuse. 'Just for a quick coffee, you understand,' he pressed. 'I've got a full afternoon's list and you're probably rushing off somewhere.'

'Well, I suppose I could spare a few minutes,' she said, torn between conflicting emotions. 'I'll wait there for you.'

'Great,' said Andrew, adding under his breath, 'In case you've forgotten, mine's a regular coffee, no sugar.' He gave her a wicked look before turning to the patient.

When she'd left the room, he forced himself to concentrate on the patient even though thoughts of Helen kept intruding, making his mind wander. He was just so happy to have found her, he couldn't stop smiling.

'Mr Birdwell,' he said, grinning from ear to ear, 'tell me about your knee…'

Helen walked quickly down the corridor, wondering if she'd bitten off more than she was prepared to chew.

She went into the canteen and bought two coffees, taking them to a table as far away from the main area as possible. She had no idea what she and Andrew were going to be saying to each other, but she knew she didn't want their conversation to be overheard by a roomful of hospital staff.

Helen checked her watch at least a dozen times in as many minutes. Her mother might be wondering what was keeping her late, although she knew well enough that her daughter could often be delayed by patients needing urgent attention. Helen was wondering whether she should give her mother a quick phone call when Andrew walked in. He looked around the room and soon spotted her, then walked over to the table briskly.

'That took me longer than anticipated,' he said. 'Our Mr Birdwell is going to need arthroscopic treatment on his knee and I've managed to slot him in at the front of my operating list tomorrow.'

He sat down facing her. 'Is this for me?' he asked, taking the lid off the paper cup.

'It's probably cold by now,' said Helen, grateful to be able to chat about unimportant things, like whether or not the coffee was drinkable, instead of…well, instead of going straight into a serious and, no doubt, emotional conversation.

'Coffee's fine,' said Andrew, sipping the lukewarm liquid. He felt his hands shaking and gripped the cup to stop it spilling out. Now that he was finally with her, he was finding it difficult to choose the right words to say.

'How long are you over here?' she asked, still reeling from the shock of seeing him in Milchester.

'I'm on a six-month contract,' he said, then, relaxing a little, grinned happily, adding, 'It's so good to see you. I was really quite surprised, and delighted, to find you working here.'

'I was pretty surprised to find you here, I must say.'

She glanced at her watch once again. 'Anyway, I can't stay long. I have to…be somewhere soon. I only work here part time.'

She almost said *I have to go home to my baby* but she instinctively stopped herself in time. She had no idea what they were going to be talking about in the next few minutes, but she knew one item that was not going to be discussed—and that was Robert. She'd decided that this was definitely not the right time or place to tell Andrew that he had a baby son.

'So,' said Andrew, 'I thought you might possibly be working somewhere that specialises in sports medicine.'

'No,' she said, 'not at the moment. Although that is my ultimate aim, of course.'

'That's what I thought,' he replied. 'In fact, I was amazed to discover that you had left New York. I was convinced you were going to be working there in sports medicine. I seem to remember you were offered a very good job…'

'I was,' she cut in quickly. 'I changed my mind. Got homesick.'

'Ah, yes,' he said, nodding his head slowly. 'That's what the professor implied.'

'The professor?' This was news to Helen.

'I spoke to him about you when I returned from Chicago. I tried to contact you in New York but you'd left. I eventually discovered you'd gone home to England but old Mulberry wouldn't give me your address. He said he believed you had a boyfriend.' said Andrew, gripping his paper cup tightly. 'He said that

was why you went home…to be with this boyfriend
in England.'

'Oh,' said Helen.

A silence opened up between them like a chasm.
Eventually Andrew spoke. 'Was he correct?'

'He might have been,' said Helen, determined to
give very little away about her private life.

Andrew reached across and took hold of her left
hand, scrutinising it.

'You're not married to him, though, are you?' he
said, commenting on the lack of rings on her third
finger.

'I'm not married yet.' She pulled her hand away.

'Yet?' His heart skipped a beat. 'You mean there
is someone?'

Helen looked away and into the far corner of the
room.

'Yes,' she said eventually. 'We're getting married
quite soon.'

His spirits sank into his boots. So, that was that,
was it? He'd come all this way, got a job in a town
he didn't know, just to try and find Helen…and now
he discovered he was too late! He swallowed the cold
coffee. Hang on a minute, don't despair, he urged
himself. The woman's not married yet—there's still
a chance she could change her mind…or be per-
suaded to change her mind.

'You could still come out with me for a meal one
night, couldn't you? For old times' sake? Your fiancé
wouldn't object to that, I'm sure.'

Andrew fixed her with one of his mesmerising
looks. She realised, with a sense of deepening reality,
that he was beginning to work his magic on her. Her

resolution just to have a coffee and then have nothing more to do with him was beginning to weaken.

'Possibly,' she said. 'I'm just not sure when I'm free…'

'Tonight?'

'Not tonight.'

'Tomorrow, then?'

Helen rose from the table and picked up her bag. 'Andrew, I'm just not sure about it, that's all.'

'What's there to be sure about?'

'Well,' she began, 'for a start you disappear out of my life and go to Chicago, and then you suddenly reappear—'

'I can explain all about that.'

'And I'm not sure if Patrick will be understanding if I go out with you one evening.'

'Patrick?'

'The man I'm going to marry.'

Andrew drummed his fingers on the Formica table and looked up at her, giving her his most persuasive smile. 'Surely he'll understand if you tell him you're just going out with an old friend, a medical colleague, who's over from the States and who's going back in a few months' time?'

She hesitated for a moment and then moved away from the table. This time she wasn't going to let him persuade her to act against her better judgement. She shook her head.

'I don't think it's a good idea. And now I have to go,' she said. 'I'll see you around, possibly.'

She walked briskly to the canteen door, not daring to look back. When she was sitting in her mother's car in the hospital car park she realised her hands were shaking so much she could hardly manage to put the key in the ignition.

Helen's mother, Dorothy, was in the kitchen, giving Robert his feed, when Helen arrived home.

'Everything all right, love?' asked her mother. 'You look a bit drained.'

'I'm fine,' she replied, stroking the baby on his soft, downy head. Then, sitting down at the kitchen table, she blurted out, 'I saw him today! That new orthopaedic surgeon…it *is* Andrew!'

Her mother took a sharp breath. 'Goodness me,' she said. 'Did you speak to him?'

Helen nodded. 'We had a quick coffee in the canteen.'

'What did he say when you told him about the baby?'

Helen tensed her lips. 'I didn't. I *know* I'm going to have to tell him, especially now that he's over here, but I just couldn't bring myself to mention it in the hospital canteen. It didn't seem the right time or the right place.'

She sat down and buried her head in her hands. 'Oh, Mum, I'm just so muddled about everything! When I saw him today it brought back all the conflicting emotions, all the torment I've been through in the past year. I do love him, that will never change. But Andrew isn't a man I could really trust, not after the way he behaved. And now I haven't just got myself to think of, there's little Robert. Thanks to Patrick, I now have the chance of a reasonably happy life with a man I'm very fond of, even though I know I can never love him the way I loved Andrew. I'm not going to risk losing all that for the sake of another one-night fling with him.'

'Is that what he suggested?' Her mother frowned.

'Not in as many words,' said Helen, smiling ruefully. 'He put it more delicately, of course, asking me out for a meal one evening.'

'And you turned him down, I hope?'

Helen nodded mutely.

Mrs Talbot carried on feeding Robert, talking to him softly. 'Good boy…nearly finished…just a few more drops.' She put the bottle down and put Robert over her left shoulder, patting him gently to bring up any air he might have taken in with the milk. She looked across at Helen.

'Did he say why he's over here?'

Helen shook her head. 'No. All he said was that he's on a six-month contract at the hospital. I expect he's planning to go back to America when that's finished. No doubt he thought he'd try and catch up with me while he was over here.' She spread her hands out on the pine table. 'I'm beginning to get a more complete picture of the guy. He flits around from town to town, country to country, picking up relationships all over the place. I was just unfortunate to be one of his many women. He should have been a sailor, not a surgeon…at least sailors are expected to have a girl in every port!'

Robert gave a loud and very satisfying burp. Both women laughed.

'Yes, Robert,' said Helen, taking him from her mother. 'That's exactly what I think of your father, too.'

*   *   *

A few days later, Andrew was on his way to the open access unit, hoping he might bump into Helen again.

Even after meeting her earlier in the week, he was still no closer to finding out her address. He was sure that if he turned up at her house one day over the weekend he might find her in a more receptive mood. He decided to try getting her home number through the hospital, and the open access unit was his starting point.

As he walked along the long corridor leading to the unit he realised how desperate he was to make contact with Helen again, and the sooner the better. He needed to find out if there was any chance at all that they could resume their affair, an affair that he'd been forced to put on hold for several months while he'd sorted things out in Chicago. Explaining his strange behaviour to Helen over a five-minute cup of coffee in a crowded hospital canteen wasn't ideal…and he had no intention of rushing it. Added to which, he'd been so taken aback and demoralised to discover that she was planning to marry someone else that he honestly didn't know what had hit him. Now that he'd had time to gather his thoughts together he felt he was better prepared to start winning her back again.

In the open access unit he was disappointed, but not surprised, to find that she wasn't there. She'd told him that she only worked there part time.

'Hello, Dr Henderson,' said the desk clerk, 'can I help you?'

'I was wondering if you had Dr Blackburn's home address? She brought a patient across to me earlier in the week and I—'

Before he could finish his explanation, the desk

clerk was looking up the required information on the computer.

'Sure, Dr Henderson,' she said. 'Just hang on a minute and I'll find it for you. Dr Helen Blackburn?'

'That's right,' replied Andrew.

'Here it is. I'll write it down for you.' She scribbled three or four lines on a notepad, tore off the sheet and handed it to him.

'Many thanks,' he said, taking the note and putting it in his pocket.

CHAPTER SEVEN

ON SUNDAY afternoon, Andrew cancelled the game of tennis he'd previously arranged with a work colleague. He couldn't settle to doing anything until he'd got his visit to Helen organised. He couldn't put it off any longer. The sooner the two of them talked things over, the sooner he could get his life in order once again.

Why was everything so complicated? Why had the Chicago fiasco had to happen just at a time when he'd met the most exciting woman who'd come into his life for years?

He opened his map of Milchester, folding it in four so that it showed the area he needed…the road where Helen lived. As a stranger to the town he needed to study it carefully while he planned the route.

When he had familiarised himself with where he was going, he picked up his keys and stepped out of his rented house into the brightness of the warm June day.

It didn't take him long to reach her road as it was only a few miles from the city centre. It was in a quiet suburban setting, a little oasis off the main thoroughfare into town, with tree-lined streets and a small park nearby. There were dozens of cars parked on both sides of the road. Andrew drove past them slowly, counting the house numbers as he searched for number 29. When he had located it he had a problem finding a space and ended up parking a long way from the house.

'Must be a party going on at one of the houses,' he muttered to himself as he walked towards number 29. It hadn't occurred to him for one minute that the party would be at the house he was heading for. It wasn't until he rang the doorbell that he realised that the party was indeed at Helen's house.

The door was opened by a woman he vaguely recognised, dressed in an elegant summer dress and jacket. There was a lot of noise in the background. He was struck by doubt.

'I'm sorry,' he said. 'I think I must have got the wrong house.'

'Dr Henderson!' said the woman, her face a curious mix of expressions—surprise, momentary pleasure, then serious concern. He still couldn't recall where he'd seen her before.

'You know me?' He was baffled and a little bemused.

'I work at the hospital,' she said. 'I'm Dorothy Talbot…Nurse Talbot.'

'Ah!' said Andrew. 'I was wondering where I'd seen you before. I've obviously come to the wrong house. I'm looking for the house where Helen Blackburn lives…Dr Blackburn.'

Another expression replaced the earlier one. This time her face went hard, her mouth set tight. She spoke almost in a whisper. 'What do you want? Why are you here?'

'I told you, Mrs Talbot,' Andrew replied with a light laugh. 'I'm looking for Helen, but I seem to have come to the wrong house, although…' He checked the piece of paper where the address had been written for him. 'I'm looking for number 29 and I could have sworn that this was the house!'

'It is,' said Dorothy Talbot not moving an inch, not opening the door any wider. 'And, yes, this is where Helen lives.' She looked like thunder.

Andrew was relieved to at least have tracked Helen down, but didn't know why this woman, a nurse he now discovered, had turned into a dragon.

'Could I have a quick word with her, do you think? I won't keep her a minute because I can see there's obviously some sort of party going on.'

'She's busy. It's not convenient now.' She made to close the door. Andrew decided to do something he'd only seen done in the movies or on TV. He put his foot in the door.

'I'm sorry to behave like this, Mrs Talbot, but I think you should at least speak to Helen while I'm here. Are you her landlady or something?' He kept his voice calm but assertive.

'I'm her mother,' said the dragon lady. 'And I'd just like to tell you that Helen is happy and I think you should leave her alone. Please, remove your foot from the door.'

'Now, just a minute—' Before he could finish the sentence someone else joined in the conversation, someone he couldn't see but whose voice was instantly recognisable.

'What's going on, Mum? Why don't you come into the garden? Patrick's waiting for you so he can make his speech.'

'Helen? Is that you?' he called out.

'Andrew?'

Helen stood behind her mother in the doorway. Her mother opened the door wider and then, stepping to the side, walked away, whispering something to Helen as she went.

Helen was holding a baby in a long white robe.

'Oh, hi!' said Andrew. 'I guess I've come at a bad time. Is there some sort of christening party going on?'

'Yes.' Her face was a blank.

Andrew peered at the baby.

'Nice kid. Boy or girl?'

'Boy.'

'Are you his godmother?' Andrew asked.

Helen didn't answer immediately but stared at him for several seconds before dropping her gaze to the baby.

'I'm his mother.'

It was a good thing that Andrew had previously removed his foot from the doorway because he needed both feet firmly planted on the ground to stop himself from falling over.

'His *mother*? You've got a *baby*?' Andrew hoped he didn't look as foolish as he knew he must sound. 'I mean…I didn't know.'

'I don't suppose you did,' said Helen, undecided how to handle the situation. She still wasn't sure whether Andrew realised the baby was his. But from the way he was looking at her it was obvious that he had come to another conclusion entirely…a conclusion she was more than happy for him to jump to at this particularly inconvenient moment.

At that moment someone else appeared at the doorway, a thin, red-haired man with glasses. Andrew estimated him to be in his late thirties or early forties.

'Are you coming, Helen?' the man asked. 'First of all your mother disappears and now you and the baby. I'm all set to make my ''wetting the baby's head'' speech, so...' He noticed Andrew standing outside. 'Another guest?'

'Andrew,' said Helen, deciding she'd better make formal introductions, 'this is my fiancé, Dr Patrick Perrott.' Turning to Patrick, she said, 'this is Dr Andrew Henderson...we were medical colleagues in New York. Dr Henderson is on a short-term contract at Milchester General.'

Patrick beamed and held out his hand. 'Delighted to meet you, Andrew. Do come in and join in the fun.'

Before either Helen or Andrew could protest, Patrick had taken Andrew by the arm and pulled him into the house. 'Follow me,' he said. 'It's all happening outside in the garden. Grab a glass of champagne and hold it in readiness for the end of my speech...which won't be too long if only I can get it started. Chance would be a fine thing!'

Andrew and Helen followed him through the patio doors and into the throng of people congregating in the garden. The dragon lady was there, he noted, giving him piercing looks from across the flower-beds. What had he done to offend the woman? Was it because she imagined he was trying to gatecrash the party or was it because he was dressed in an open-neck shirt and jeans? That was probably it. No doubt she would think he was lowering the tone of the occasion.

Patrick's speech was, as promised, short and to the point. The baby, apparently christened Robert Patrick, was toasted by everyone and wished a happy, healthy and long life. Patrick had his arm around Helen, who was holding the baby. They looked a happy couple…a happy family. Black images filled Andrew's mind. Jealousy, anger, frustration and more than a little self-pity came over him in great waves. He downed his champagne and headed for the patio doors, determined to leave before he said or did anything he'd later regret.

'Dr Henderson!' someone called out.

He turned and saw a young woman waving from the other side of the lawn. She was running towards him. He recognised her. It was a doctor he'd worked with in the ER in New York. She'd been Helen's flatmate, he recalled…Jane, he remembered, was her name.

'Hi!' she said breathlessly. 'I didn't know you were coming to the christening. I'm the godmother. I flew in from the States this morning and I'm still suffering from jet-lag!'

'Great,' said Andrew. 'Nice to see you again. I have to be going. I only called in for a moment to see Helen.'

'Is this the first time you've seen the baby?' Jane asked, unsure how much he knew.

'Yes. He's a little trouper, isn't he? But he hasn't got his dad's red hair.' Andrew glanced across at where Helen and Patrick were standing. The baby was being handed around various admiring people.

'Er…yes,' said Jane. 'You mean Patrick?'

'Who else?' Andrew paused before walking to the

front door. 'Anyway, nice to see you again, Jane. Safe journey back.'

He let himself out and walked back to where he'd parked his car. He couldn't wait to get away from the place. He'd come to England on a six-month contract with the express aim of wooing and winning Helen…and he was too late. When he'd talked to her in the hospital canteen and he'd been told the black news that she was going to marry another man—that had been bad enough. But at least he'd been left with a tiny bit of hope. If she hadn't actually married the man, Andrew had felt that he'd been in with a fighting chance of getting her back, of making her change her mind. But now…now he'd discovered that they had a baby!

It really was too late. Helen and Patrick and their baby were a family—and Andrew had no intention of even trying to come between them. He sighed deeply and regretfully. Now it really was all over and his dreams of a life with Helen had been shattered. He couldn't wait for the remaining time to be up so he could return to the States and pick up the remnants of his medical career.

Helen noticed Andrew's departure and wasn't sure whether she was pleased or not. It was perhaps just as well he'd gone, otherwise he might have started asking awkward questions about Robert's age—and then working out for himself that he was the father.

Jane came over and told her of the short conversation she'd had with him.

'He's convinced that Patrick is Robert's father. I didn't know what to say.'

Helen's eyes grew round. 'You didn't tell him?'

'No, of course not. I was just very surprised to see him here.'

'You and me both,' said Helen ruefully. 'I nearly dropped the baby with shock when I saw him standing on the doorstep, talking to Mum.'

'Don't you think it's a bit…' Jane screwed up her face '…*mean* not letting him know he's Robert's father. He has that basic human right, surely?'

'He has no rights whatsoever where Robert's concerned! You know that, Jane! When he left me and buzzed off to Chicago, he forfeited any rights he ever had.' Helen's voice was bitter and angry. 'I shall tell him when I'm ready to do so. That's *my* basic human right!'

'Of course,' said Jane to pacify her. 'Now, how about another glass of champers? Patrick is opening bottles by the dozen so come on, let's party!'

CHAPTER EIGHT

IN THE weeks since the christening, Helen didn't see Andrew on any of the days she'd been working at the open access unit. She did wonder if he was being kept very busy in Orthopaedics—but she also wondered if he was deliberately avoiding her.

She had given a lot of thought to how and when she should tell Andrew about the baby. She'd worked out when his contract would come to an end and planned to tell him just before he went back to America. But she kept having doubts and guilty feelings about keeping Robert's parentage a secret from Andrew. Her conversation with Jane was weighing heavily on her conscience and she decided she had to tell him now. But what was the best way to do it? Write him a letter? Or tell him face to face? She asked her mother for advice.

'I'd write to him, if I were you,' Dorothy said. 'That way you can spend some time choosing exactly the right words. It's not something you can just go up to a man and tell him right in his face! I know some women do that, but I always think it's kinder to let the man have a bit of privacy when he first hears that kind of news.'

'You don't think it's cowardly just to write a letter?' asked Helen nervously.

'No, dear,' said her mother. 'You can say in the

letter that you're very happy to talk it over with him—or words to that effect.'

Helen hesitated for a moment. 'I don't know his home address.'

'Then send to him at the hospital,' said Dorothy firmly. 'Mark it private and confidential.'

When Andrew received the letter, his reaction was one of sheer fury. He marched over to the open access unit, only to find it closed.

'Have you seen Dr Blackburn?' he asked a nurse.

'She hasn't been in today,' he was told.

Driving through busy city traffic, he nevertheless managed to reach her home in less than fifteen minutes. He spotted her getting out of a red Metro, carrying several supermarket shopping bags. He parked nearby and strode purposefully over to her.

Helen saw him walking toward her. He looked like thunder. She felt sick with nerves.

'How could you do it?' he said between clenched teeth. 'How could you deceive me like this?'

'What do you mean?' said Helen weakly.

'What do you think you're playing at?' He hadn't raised his voice, but the quiet, angry way he spoke sent a chill through her. 'Why didn't you tell me right at the start that the baby was mine?'

'I did what I did for the best,' she said, trying to keep her cool. Andrew had thrown her on the defensive and she was finding it very hard to gain the upper ground.

He pointed an accusing finger at her. 'You had no right to do what you did. No right to come back to England, knowing you were pregnant with my child and not even telling me! How do you think that makes me feel?'

Helen closed her eyes for a brief moment, summoning up her assertiveness. 'Frankly, Andrew, I don't care how it makes you feel. I wrote and told you that you are Robert's father because I felt you had a right to know.'

'You're dead right I have! You're a bitch, do you know that?' His face was contorted with anger.

Her heart was pounding but she was determined not to let him browbeat her. His extreme reaction had taken her unawares. She'd thought he might be cross for being kept in the dark about being a father but, considering that he appeared to have other plans for his life that didn't include her, he was definitely over-reacting. She sensed that it was his pride that had been hurt more than anything. He must have hated being kept in the dark. Well, that was all in the past and she had to consider her own future and, of course, Robert's.

'Would you, please, leave?' she said calmly.

'This is a public road and I most certainly will not leave. Not until you tell me what your plans are for bringing up my son.'

'He will be brought up by Patrick and me,' she said. 'What else did you expect?'

'In that case, I must tell you that you'll both be hearing from my lawyers.'

Helen laughed at the notion. 'Your lawyers can't stop me marrying Patrick—or anyone else I choose to marry!'

'I'm talking about my son,' said Andrew. 'I shall be demanding access and all other parental rights.'

She was temporarily speechless.

'You've not heard the last from me, Dr Blackburn. You can run away from me but you can't deny me my son!'

Helen's pulse was racing furiously. 'The sooner you get back to America the better! Chicago, New York, wherever you like…but just go!'

'I'm going back, don't worry about that. But I might very well be taking Robert with me. I shall be applying for custody and I believe I'm in a very favourable position to get it! Goodbye, Helen.'

He walked back to his car and drove away loudly.

She was gripped by a clammy fear. Andrew couldn't take away her baby, could he? The idea was so ridiculous she almost laughed. Nevertheless, it was a few moments before she composed herself and walked to her front door.

The following day Helen still hadn't come to terms with the confrontation outside the house. She couldn't decide what had upset her most—Andrew's threat to cause trouble over access to Robert or the way he'd turned his anger on her.

It was a lovely summer's day and Helen was pushing Robert in his baby buggy towards the little park. He was lying flat on his back fast asleep with the most angelic look on his face.

'My little cherub,' whispered Helen to him as they neared the park entrance. There were children playing on the swings, and three other mothers with babies in buggies.

She found an empty bench in a shady spot and sat

down, keeping one hand on the buggy and rocking it gently.

Try as she might, she couldn't wipe from her mind the picture of Andrew and the bitter way he'd spoken to her the previous day. Tears began to spring into her eyes once again and she wiped them away briskly. She couldn't stop herself from wanting to burst into tears every time she thought about it. Her mother had been most concerned when Helen, returning with her shopping, had walked into the kitchen with tears streaming down her face.

She'd told her mother what had just happened and almost immediately regretted doing so. Her mother had flown into a rage and called Jack into the kitchen. The two of them had proceeded to outline a plan of defence in, as Jack put it, 'the unlikely event' that Andrew would carry out his threat.

She'd hardly slept a wink last night as she'd gone over, time and time again, her conversation with Andrew. She blew her nose and stared out across the park, feeling wretched. She was startled from her reverie by a familiar voice behind her.

'Hayfever?' he asked. 'There's quite a lot of it about this year, so I've heard.'

'Andrew!' She looked round and there he was standing next to the buggy. He was wearing chinos and a blue open-necked shirt.

He sat down next to her. 'I had to speak to you. About yesterday.'

Helen's defence mechanism kicked in. 'You've not come to try and take Robert, have you? Because if you have—'

He put a reassuring hand on her. 'No. I've come to apologise.'

'Oh.'

He took the wind out of her sails, but still the scene of yesterday's confrontation played itself in her head.

'I shouldn't have said what I did.' His handsome, serious face was close to hers.

'So you're not going to try and take Robert away?' She was wary. Once again she felt herself on the brink of tears and her eyes began to fill up.

'No,' he said. 'I don't know what made me say that. Anger, frustration perhaps. Or maybe it was just the shock of realising that the baby was mine.'

Tears spilled from her eyes. He turned her face to his and gently stroked her cheek dry with his fingers. 'I'm sorry for upsetting you so much.'

The gentleness in his voice and the conciliatory tone of his voice touched her deep inside and made her realise that his apology was genuine.

Andrew was now standing by the buggy, looking at the baby. The soft expression on his face moved Helen so much that she thought she was going to blub again.

'He's lovely,' said Andrew, leaning over the buggy as Robert began to stir. 'He's waking up. Hello, young fellow. You're a handsome chap, aren't you?'

Robert gave him a gummy smile and began to kick his legs and wave his arms excitedly.

Andrew turned to Helen. 'May I pick him up?'

'Sure. Help yourself.' She bit her lip. She realised she must have sounded flippant when inside she was a mass of deep emotions. Her baby was going to be held for the first time by his father, and she'd just answered as if someone had asked to borrow a pencil!

He picked up Robert as if he were handling the Crown Jewels. The ecstatic look on Andrew's face as he held his son, cradling him in the crook of his arm, was an image that would always stay with Helen.

He said nothing for a long time and just rocked Robert gently to and fro, gazing at him intently as if he wanted to imprint this moment on his memory for ever.

Eventually, without taking his eyes from his son, he asked Helen, 'Why did you call him Robert?'

'It was my father's name,' she answered.

Andrew continued rocking his son. 'It was my father's name, too,' he said.

'Ah. Is it? Was it?' Helen frowned. 'I didn't know.'

'No reason why you should. But it's a nice omen, don't you think?'

Helen's frown deepened. 'How do you mean?'

'Both Robert's grandfathers had the same name, the name that he has. It's a good omen for his future, a sort of lucky sign.'

With obvious reluctance, Andrew lowered the baby back into his buggy. The little arms waved about wildly. Andrew caught hold of Robert's tiny hands in his.

'I think you're going to have a lot of luck on your side, big boy.'

Robert chuckled.

'Are you coming to the hospital dance next week?' Andrew asked out of the blue.

'Dance? Oh, the fund-raising thing?' Helen remembered seeing posters around the hospital and had heard several of the staff talking about it. 'I might,' she said, adding hastily, '...we might. I mentioned it to Patrick and he seemed keen.'

She deliberately threw in Patrick's name to see what kind of response she'd get from Andrew. It was her way of testing whether he was genuinely remorseful over the way he'd threatened legal action over access to Robert.

The mention of Patrick's name passed without comment and Andrew continued to play with the baby. Whenever he let go of one of the tiny hands, Robert would stick out his bottom lip and look as if he was about to cry.

'I can see I'm going to have to stand here all day with you, young man, or I'll end up making you cry. And that's something I have no intention of doing.'

'It's getting near his feeding time,' interjected Helen. 'Don't be thinking it's you who's making him cry.'

Andrew let go of the baby's hands. Robert cried for a few moments before the rocking motion of the buggy calmed him down.

'We must go,' said Helen.

'Me, too,' said Andrew. He looked longingly into the buggy. 'See you again soon, I hope.'

Helen wasn't sure to whom he was addressing the remark, herself or the baby. She answered for them both.

'Yes, see you again soon.' She added, 'You can see Robert whenever you want. I'm not going to stop you.'

He kissed her fleetingly on the cheek. 'Bless you for that.' And then he was gone.

Robert was beginning to grizzle for his feed and she walked home as quickly as she could.

She had found the meeting with Andrew thrilling, moving and distressing in equal measure. She was thrilled to see him—because he always had that effect on her. But she also found it heart-achingly moving, watching the loving way he'd held his small son for the very first time. And the whole encounter had distressed her in a way that she just couldn't explain— all she knew was that her legs were feeling decidedly wobbly and she was completely drained emotionally and physically.

When Helen and Patrick arrived at the hospital for the fund-raising dance it was well under way.

The lecture theatre had been converted for the evening into a dance hall and couples were gyrating to the pacy rhythm of the 1960s-style band. The female vocalist, a very attractive girl, whom Helen thought she'd seen before but couldn't remember where, was belting out her version of a popular Beatles' song.

Helen scanned the crowd and recognised many of the faces.

'Glad you made it, Dr Blackburn,' said Shirley, the desk clerk. 'It's a really great band, don't you think?'

'Sounds good to me,' replied Helen. 'The singer's good, too.'

'You know who that is, don't you? It's Margie Whittaker, one of the theatre sisters. We don't normally get to see her with her hair down!'

Patrick's eyes had been glued on Margie, Helen noted, ever since they'd walked in the room. Could it have something to do with her shoulder-length auburn hair? she wondered, smiling inwardly.

'Come on, Patrick,' she urged. 'Take your eyes off the singer and have a dance with me!'

They joined the heaving throng, their arms around each other as they got into the rhythm and beat.

'The surgeons will be looking at Margie with new eyes from now on,' she said, raising her voice to make herself heard above the din.

'Yes,' said Patrick, trying to concentrate on his footwork, which was difficult for him as he was also watching the vocalist who was tossing her fiery tresses as she reached the climax of the song.

As the music ended the dancers drifted slowly from the dance floor. Helen was glad of the excuse to stop dancing with Patrick. Maybe it was because his mind was elsewhere, but he definitely didn't seem to have a natural sense of rhythm the way she remembered that Andrew had when they'd danced together in Seattle.

Damn, damn, damn, she thought. I must stop comparing Patrick with Andrew, and I must stop thinking about Andrew all the time.

But even as the resolve formed itself in her mind, the man himself walked into the room, banishing all chances of her keeping her resolution.

She could see him casting his eyes around the room until he saw her. He gave a small wave, which she returned before turning her back on him and talking animatedly to Patrick.

'So, do you do a lot of dancing?' she asked him brightly, even though the soreness of her feet could have given her a clue to the answer.

'I'm afraid not,' he said ruefully. 'My mother offered to pay for dancing lessons when I was a teenager but none of my friends were going and I just knew I'd be mocked and called a sissy. I'm sorry now that I didn't take her up on the offer.'

'Well, you know what my old granny used to say— men who are good dancers make the worst husbands.' Helen chuckled as she said it, smiling a false, hard smile mainly for the benefit of Andrew who, she was convinced, was watching her from across the room.

'Your old granny was wrong in my case,' said Patrick. 'I'm a lousy dancer and I didn't make a very good husband either. But I'm determined to do better next time.'

Helen, realising she may have put her foot in it, squeezed his arm companionably.

'Everyone's allowed to make one mistake, I always say. And your dancing isn't too bad,' she lied kindly.

'In that case, let's give it another try.' Patrick took her hand and led her to the dance floor as the band struck up a familiar rock 'n' roll number.

Patrick's idea of how to jive was almost as bad as his dancing had been before. Several times Helen ended up with her arms twisted behind her back in a fierce armlock. On one occasion she actually cried out in pain when she narrowly avoided having her elbow dislocated.

During the evening she noticed that Andrew wasn't dancing but was spending most of his time chatting to one of the other surgeons.

Patrick went to the bar to get some more drinks and Helen decided to pay a visit to the powder room. On the way back she looked around the crowded room for Patrick but couldn't immediately see him. As she was hesitating and wondering where to wait for him, Andrew walked up to her.

'Hi,' he said. His eyes travelled over her body and the clingy aquamarine silk sleeveless dress that was slit to the knee. 'You look great.'

'Thanks,' she replied lightly. Then the band struck up again, drowning his next words.

'What did you say?' she asked.

He moved closer and spoke into her ear. 'I said it's hot in here.'

'Yes,' she shouted back. She looked down the dance floor, trying to locate Patrick.

'Lost your boyfriend?' asked Andrew, raising his voice to make himself heard.

'He went to get some drinks,' replied Helen, still searching for him.

'There he is.' Andrew pointed towards the band area.

There was now a male vocalist taking the place of Margie whom Helen surmised was taking a break. When Helen looked in the direction Andrew was pointing she saw Patrick deep in conversation with the 'resting' Margie. Helen started to push her way towards him when Andrew put a restraining hand on her.

'Don't spoil his fun,' he said. 'Come and have a drink with me instead. You can trust him to talk to another woman for a few minutes, can't you?'

She didn't want Andrew to think that she didn't trust the man she was about to marry. 'Of course I can,' she said defensively.

She followed him out of the hot, noisy hall and

into the relative calm of the bar, a room that was normally the staff canteen. He took her hand and carried on walking through the bar and out into the warm night air.

'I thought you were getting me a drink?' said Helen.

'All in good time,' he said, pulling her to him as he leaned against the outside wall. Light was spilling out of the canteen but he'd managed to position them both in semi-darkness away from prying eyes.

He put his arm round her, pulling her gently towards him. She could feel his heart pounding and a tremor raced through her body.

'You're not really going to marry him, are you?' he whispered against her ear.

'Yes,' she replied. 'He loves me and—'

Before she could finish the sentence Andrew kissed her, his mouth tantalisingly soft and tormenting. She was powerless to resist and she responded to him, hating herself for being so weak.

'He may love you,' he said huskily into her ear, 'but I don't think you love him.'

'You can't possibly know that,' she replied breathlessly, arching her back as he ran his hand down her spine, pressing her body to his.

'I've seen the way you are with him. Your whole body language shrieks it. Shrieks that you don't love him.'

Andrew kissed her again—on her face, on her neck—moving her hair to one side and running his mouth and tongue hotly and sensually over her skin.

Helen moaned with pleasure, longing for him to

continue and at the same time longing for him to stop! She shook herself free.

'Patrick loves me and we're getting married and there's nothing you can do to stop us!'

Andrew stood back, leaning against the wall, folding his arms. A half-smile was visible in the shadowy light.

'You say he loves you…then why is he so busy chatting up that redhead in there?' He jerked his head in the direction of the music.

Helen had a quick response on her lips, but before she could get it out the word 'redhead' struck a blow. It was true Patrick had been very interested in Margie from the moment he'd first seen her. Was she fooling herself that Patrick was capable of putting all that behind him when they married or would he always be vulnerable to glamorous redheads? It wasn't a prospect she relished and it didn't bode well for the future success of their marriage.

When she didn't answer, Andrew reached out and pulled her to him again.

'We need to clear the air,' he said. 'There are things I have to talk to you about but this isn't the place to do it. Come back to my house. It's not far away.'

'I can't leave Patrick here,' she said.

'Then go and tell him,' suggested Andrew. 'Tell him you'll be back in an hour or so.'

Helen laughed at the idea. 'I can't do that!'

He cupped her face in his hands and kissed her gently on the lips. 'You said you trusted him—let's see if he trusts you.'

He could sense she was weakening but hadn't made

up her mind to come home with him. And he needed her to do so very much. He wanted to test whether or not he was still in with a chance of winning her back or whether she truly did love Patrick. He might end up getting his face slapped but it was a risk worth taking.

'Please,' he said. 'It's very important—for me. I'm having to return to America at the end of my contract because I've already signed up for another job. But I'm planning to come back again so that I can be with my son. So you see, there are important things we have to discuss about Robert. We need a bit of privacy.'

Helen knew he was using every weapon in his armoury to get his own way. It was the mention of Robert's name that decided her-and the fact that he was planning on coming back to England because of the baby.

'OK,' she said. 'I'll go and find Patrick and tell him.'

She made her way back to the dance floor, Andrew following closely behind. She scanned it but couldn't see Patrick. She looked in the corner near where the band was playing and where she'd last seen him talking to Margie, and he wasn't there either. He wasn't anywhere to be seen…and neither was Margie.

'Why don't you leave a note for him with someone?' suggested Andrew.

After a few minutes Helen decided that this was the best course of action. She scribbled a note for him, saying that she'd be back before the end of the dance. She sought out Shirley and said to her, 'You know Dr Perrott, don't you?' Helen handed Shirley the note, saying, 'When you see him, can you give him this, please? I've been called away for a short time and I don't want him worrying about me.'

'Sure, Dr Blackburn,' said Shirley, taking the note and putting it in her handbag.

Andrew drove the short distance to his rented house and parked outside.

He held Helen's hand as they walked up the path and continued holding it even while he unlocked the front door.

When they were inside the house he pulled her to him once again and they stayed kissing in the hallway for several minutes.

'I thought we were meant to be talking,' she said breathlessly.

'Plenty of time for that,' he replied, sliding his hands round the back of her dress, finding the zipper.

Her whole body tingled with excitement and the anticipation of his exploring hands, recalling their previous physical encounter and the complete and utter pleasure he'd been able to give her. No other man had even come close; no other man could make love to her like he could. Helen realised she was in danger of acting foolishly, and not for the first time where Andrew was concerned, but she couldn't help herself. It was as if she was totally mesmerised by him.

'Helen, you know that I love you, don't you?'

'Do you?' she said breathlessly between kisses. 'Do you really?'

'Let me show you how much,' he said huskily, his hands all over her.

In a state of half-undress—Helen in lacy bra and

pants, Andrew in shirt and boxer shorts—he picked
her up and carried her to the bedroom.

Just as he placed her on the bed the phone rang.

The strident ringing shocked Helen into reacting
instinctively and she automatically reached out and
picked up the phone which was on the bedside table
nearest to her.

'Dr Blackburn,' she said, then, putting a hand over
her mouth, added, 'Sorry, Dr Henderson's phone. Can
I help you?'

She realised how silly she must have sounded and
smiled. But she wasn't smiling for long, not when she
heard the sultry female voice at the other end of the
phone.

'Oh, hi,' she said. 'It's Lori Martin. I'm phoning
from Chicago and hoping to catch Andrew before it
gets too late in the day. I keep forgetting about the
time difference!' The woman gave a throaty laugh.

'Just a minute, please,' said Helen, a chill entering
her voice. 'Someone from Chicago,' she said, handing
the cordless phone to Andrew.

He sat on the edge of the bed as he took the call,
his back to Helen.

'Oh, Lori, hello.' He didn't say anything else for a
few moments but listened to what his caller had to
say. Helen's suspicions were aroused, particularly
when Andrew got up from the bed and, putting his
hand over the mouthpiece, said to her, 'I'm going to
take this call in the other room.'

She sat on the bed for a little while, all manner of
doubts passing through her mind. She went over the
facts. A woman rings Andrew from Chicago…a very
sexy-sounding woman…and he takes the call out of

her hearing. Why do that? What had he got to hide? As if she didn't know! How naïve was she? He'd told her he loved her and she'd believed him!

She got up from the bed and went in search of the rest of her clothes and her handbag. She dressed hurriedly and, hearing the sound of his voice coming from behind a closed door, let herself out of his house and walked a short distance until she could hail a taxi.

On the way back to the hospital she reflected on her romantic liaisons with Andrew and how they always seemed to end disastrously. She was furious— furious with him and even more furious with herself for getting taken in by him, not once but twice! What a fool she was!

She arrived back at the hospital in time for the last waltz. Patrick spied her walking in and came rushing across, a guilty look on his face.

'I hope you didn't go off in a huff because I was talking to that theatre sister,' he said. 'It was nothing serious, just a bit of banter.'

I'm a fine one to criticise anyone tonight, thought Helen, and she smiled at him generously.

'I didn't leave in a huff and it wasn't because of that,' she said. Taking him by the hand, she led him onto the dance floor. 'Let's have the last waltz. It's easy—just count one, two, three.'

'I think even I can manage that,' replied Patrick, relieved that Helen didn't seem put out by his little flirtation with Margie.

By her next working day at the hospital, Helen had already begun to question her own actions in relation to Andrew. Had she acted hastily on the night of the dance? Had she jumped to the wrong conclusions? After all, the phone call from Chicago could have been perfectly innocent. Perhaps she'd read too much into the fact that he'd chosen to take the call out of her hearing. It might have been a patient phoning him or, indeed, there could have been many explanations other than the one she'd chosen to believe.

She was also having serious doubts about whether she should remain engaged to Patrick. It didn't bode well for the marriage when she had been so willing to go off with another man and had almost ended up in bed with him. She also couldn't forget that Andrew, albeit in the heat of passion, had said that he loved her. Maybe he was genuine...maybe she should give him another chance.

At lunchtime she walked over to Orthopaedics. She was disappointed to find Andrew's room empty.

'Has Dr Henderson gone for lunch, do you know?' she asked the nurse on duty.

'Not yet,' she replied. 'He just popped out to see a patient on the ward. He's having lunch in his office, he said, so that he can catch up on his paperwork.'

'In that case, I'll wait in his room,' said Helen. She sat in one of his patients' chairs and idly began leafing through a medical magazine that was lying on his desk. She noticed that underneath the magazine there were several photographs.

She picked them up and saw they were all of the same person—a very glamorous blonde woman in Bermuda shorts and a sleeveless top. The background was a golf course and the pictures showed the woman in various golfing poses. She turned over the pictures to see if there was some indication of who it was. On the back of one of the photographs were the words, 'To Andrew from Lori—Happy Memories of Chicago!'

Helen looked at the pictures again, scrutinising them more closely.

So this was Lori from Chicago, was it? A very tasty piece of work with a golden tan, peroxided hair and a shapely figure.

So much for him saying that he loved her, when all along he was still in a relationship with a busty blonde from Chicago!

She tossed the pictures back on his desk in disgust and rose to leave. At that moment Andrew walked into the room. He was carrying a pack of sandwiches and a bottle of fruit juice.

'Stay for lunch, share my sandwiches?'

'No, thanks,' said Helen. 'I'm just leaving.'

He looked crestfallen. 'I'm sorry about the phone call and fully understand why you had to get back to the dance, but—'

'I fully understand, too,' she said, turning her back on him and walking to the door.

'Come out with me tonight for dinner,' he said to her retreating back. 'Will you do that?'

'No.' Her eyes blazed.

'Why not?'

'Because I don't trust you. And I don't trust myself when I'm with you.'

As he watched her walk out of his room, he had no idea what he'd done to upset her so much. He decided to cool it, to leave her be for a while. Even though she appeared determined to marry Patrick, she could never change the fact that he, Andrew Henderson, was the father of her child and, because of that, he would always be around. And, whether she trusted him or not, she'd just have to get used to it.

CHAPTER NINE

HELEN was on the afternoon shift at the open access unit.

In between seeing patients, she was chatting with one of the older nurses about Robert and the progress he'd made in just a few short months.

'Before you know it,' said the nurse, 'you'll be packing his cases and waving him off to college!'

'That seems a long way off!' Helen laughed. 'And I'm not sure if I want it to come too soon. I'm really enjoying his baby years—'

She was interrupted by her bleeper. She picked up the nearest telephone and gave her name.

'Yes, Dr Blackburn,' said the girl on the switchboard, 'there's a message for you from your mother. Can you phone home?'

Helen felt her heart miss a beat. 'Oh, I do hope nothing's happened to Robert!'

The switchboard operator wasn't able to give Helen any more details, apart from the fact that she needed to phone home.

Her hands were shaking as she dialled the number. Her mother answered straight away.

'Mum, it's me. Is everything OK with the baby?'

'Robert's fine,' said her mother. 'It's Jack. He's been injured on the golf course.'

'How?'

'I'm not sure,' replied her mother. Her voice was

anxious. 'They phoned me from the golf club to say he was being taken by ambulance to Milchester General. Can you find out what's happening? I must stay here with Robert, but as you're at the hospital anyway…'

'Yes, Mum,' said Helen, 'I'll check with A and E and go down and see him when he arrives. I'll phone you back and let you know what's happening.'

'Thanks, love.'

Helen told the desk nurse that the other two doctors in the open access unit would cover for her while she went down to find out about her stepfather.

Twenty minutes later, Helen phoned her mother to reassure her.

'He's OK,' she told Dorothy. 'He's had some sort of injury to his knee. He said it happened when he was in a bunker. He's very cross with himself because up to that moment he was winning hands down. He's had an X-ray and I'll let you know what we decide to do when we've had a look at it.'

'We?' queried her mother. 'Does that mean you'll be involved?'

'Partly,' said Helen. 'It looks as if it could be an orthopaedic injury but, of course, I won't be treating him personally, being a relative.'

'So who will treat him—Andrew Henderson? Is that what you're saying? You know I don't approve of that man because of the way he's behaved towards you.'

'If necessary,' said Helen. 'Look, Mum, if Jack has to be seen by Andrew, well, he couldn't be in better hands. If it *is* a knee injury, which I suspect it is, Andrew is the best person to deal with it.'

There was silence at the other end of the phone.

'You want Jack to have the best treatment, don't you?' said Helen.

'Of course.'

Helen replaced the receiver and went to find the emergency doctor in charge of Jack's case. So far she'd been able to keep her involvement on a purely professional level, agreeing with the A and E doctor that Jack should be seen by Dr Henderson if the X-ray confirmed her diagnosis. Relaying this information to her mother had been a little more difficult as she knew how hostile Dorothy was to the man who had, in her opinion, 'seduced and abandoned' her daughter.

'Good afternoon, Mr Talbot,' said Andrew as he entered the screened-off cubicle in A and E. He gave Helen a perfunctory nod. 'Afternoon, Dr Blackburn. And Dr Khan isn't it?'

The slim, young female SHO smiled back at him. 'Yes, Dr Henderson. I'll just take you through what's happened so far with Mr Talbot.'

Dr Khan outlined a brief history of the injury, how it had happened and the procedures and tests they'd done so far.

'The X-ray is up on the light-box,' she said. 'As far as we can see—that is, Dr Blackburn and myself—there appear to be no broken bones or dislocation.'

Andrew walked over to the light-box and studied the X-ray film.

'I think you're right, Dr Khan,' he said, pointedly addressing his remarks to the young doctor. 'Nothing appears to be broken or dislocated. We'll just take a look at the knee itself and make an assessment.'

He washed his hands and went over to the examination couch where Jack was lying.

'Mr Talbot, I'm going to examine your knee. I'll be as gentle as I can but you may experience a little discomfort as I feel around the joint.'

His fingers probed gently around the area above and below the knee joint, working his way to the knee itself. Once or twice Jack winced and said, 'Ouch.'

'Do you have any history of osteoarthritis or rheumatoid arthritis?' Andrew asked.

'No,' said Jack. 'In fact, I've never had any problem with my knees before. I hope this doesn't mean I'll be looking at trouble in the future.'

'I wouldn't have thought so,' Andrew reassured him. 'You've just damaged one of the ligaments that support the knee. After a period of rest it should return to normal.'

Jack looked relieved. 'I don't have to give up golf? I was dreading you saying that.'

'Stay off the golf course until this has healed, but after that no problem. Just avoid making any rapid twisting movements. What we're going to do now,' said Andrew, 'is to immobilise your knee for a few days and then start you on a programme of physiotherapy to strengthen the quadriceps muscle—that's the main muscle at the front of the thigh—in order to restore the blood supply to the ligament and to help it to heal.'

'Thanks,' said Jack.

'Is it still painful?' Andrew asked.

'Yes,' confirmed Jack.

'In that case,' said Andrew, 'we'll write you a pre-scription for something to ease it…and I suggest that Dr Khan gives you a painkilling injection just to see you through the immediate period. The tablets can be used after that. The injury will soon settle down once the knee is properly immobilised.'

Andrew handed Jack the prescription. 'I've made a note on your file for you to come and see me at my clinic in a week's time to check on your progress. Of course, in the meantime, if you have any problems you're in the very fortunate situation of having the expertise of Dr Blackburn on hand.' He glanced fleet-ingly at Helen before leaving the cubicle.

Jack and Helen exchanged looks but didn't say anything in front of Dr Khan. But when they were alone he said to her, 'Don't you find it awkward, working with that man? That Andrew?'

Helen shrugged. 'We're both professionals and we just get on with our jobs. Anyway, his contract at this hospital will be soon coming to an end.'

As she walked back to the open access unit Helen experienced a great wave of emotion flooding over her.

It happened every time she saw Andrew, and today was no exception. Every time she saw him she longed to touch him, to be held by him, to lose herself in his embrace. And even though she kept telling herself that it was no use, that Andrew wasn't the kind of man to commit himself to any woman on a long-term basis, she still couldn't stop herself yearning for him, wanting him more than ever.

That evening, after she'd bathed Robert and put him to bed, Helen sat alone in her room, miserable and depressed. At the hospital she'd been dismissive to Jack when he'd suggested there might be a problem working in the same environment as Andrew. The truth was that it bothered her much more than she cared to admit.

The phone rang and her mother answered it. A moment later she called up to her, 'Helen, it's for you. Jane, from Iowa.'

Helen's spirits lifted at the thought of speaking to her friend.

'Hi, Jane,' she said, picking up the extension. 'Nice to hear from you.'

'I've a small piece of news for you that may or may not mean anything,' said Jane mysteriously. 'It's about Andrew. By the way, does he know about the baby?'

'Yes, I told him,' said Helen.

'So, is everything hunky-dory between you two?'

'No.' She spoke the word with sharp vehemence.

'I thought that maybe once Andrew knew he was a father, that would change his attitude and settle him down.'

'Far from it,' said Helen. 'He's still just as uncommitted as ever. And I'm sure he has a woman in Chicago.'

'Now that you mention Chicago, that's why I'm phoning,' said Jane. 'You know how we couldn't work out the mystery behind his disappearing like that? Well, I came across a small item in an American medical journal. I'll read it to you. ''The Chicago branch of the office of professional misconduct announced that Dr Andrew Henderson has won the mal-

practice suit that was filed against him and the
Chicago City Orthopaedic Hospital.'''

'What?' said Helen. 'What's all that about?'

'I don't really know,' said Jane, 'But it seems to
me that the reason Andrew went away to Chicago last
year was to defend some sort of medical negligence
case.'

'Is there any more information in that journal?'

'Afraid not,' said Jane. 'It's on a page full of small
reports of a similar nature about doctors being struck
off or winning law suits…all that kind of thing. I just
thought you should know because it might explain
why he acted so mysteriously about Chicago.'

'But why couldn't he tell me?' said Helen. 'Didn't
he trust me enough?'

'I guess when you've got a malpractice suit hang-
ing over you, you want to keep it as quiet as possible,'
suggested Jane. 'I mean, what if he'd lost it? His career would have been in big trouble. Maybe he didn't
want to risk you being dragged down with him.'

What Jane had said made Helen thoughtful. 'Do
you think you could find out more about this malpractice thing? It could explain an awful lot.'

'I've a better idea,' said Jane. 'Why don't you just
go on over to him and ask him yourself? He might
take you out for a celebration, and who knows where
that might lead? He could turn out to be Mr
Commitment after all!'

'I doubt it.' Helen wasn't convinced.

She was very tempted to drive to his house and
confront him on the doorstep and demand to know
why he hadn't told her about his 'secret' malpractice suit.

But the more she thought about it, the more she realised that she needed to be calm when she faced him. After all, there could still be a woman in Chicago with whom he was maintaining an ongoing relationship—the glamorous golfing Lori, perhaps?

It was three days before she saw Andrew again. She'd called into the Orthopaedics department earlier in the week but had been told that he was taking a couple of days' leave.

She saw him in the staff canteen on the day he was due back and took her lunch-tray over to his table.

'Mind if I join you?' she asked.

He seemed surprised to see her. 'Not at all,' he said. 'I got the impression you were avoiding all unnecessary contact with me.'

She sat down opposite him. She decided to ignore his last remark.

'I heard from Jane Howorth a few days ago. She telephoned from America,' she said, unwrapping the Cellophane from her pre-packed sandwich. She read something out to me from an American medical journal. It was about you.'

Andrew raised a quizzical eyebrow while remaining silent.

'The item said that you'd won a medical negligence case,' said Helen.

Andrew turned to look away briefly, then faced her again.

'Yes, that right,' he said.

'But you never told me!' Helen's voice had taken on an accusing tone that she hadn't intended. 'I mean, didn't you think I'd be interested to know?' She smiled encouragingly at him. 'Do you want to talk about it now?'

'Sure,' he said, his voice giving nothing away. 'I'll tell you about it if that's what you want.'

'It's not a secret, is it? I mean, there's no reason why you shouldn't have told me?' She corrected herself so as not to seem too critical. 'I mean, is there a reason why you shouldn't tell me about it?'

Deep down she was angry with him for having kept back what must have been a very important piece of information about himself and not sharing it with her. But right now she didn't want to antagonise him in case he clammed up.

'It's not a secret,' he said. 'Not any more.'

'Not any more? But once it was?'

'Yes.' He drank his coffee. 'I wanted to tell you about it as soon as I found you over here, but events took over. The moment never seemed right.'

His bleeper went off. He laughed ruefully. 'The moment's never right for us, is it?' As he rose from the table he registered the disappointment in her face. It gave him hope, hope that she might still care a little for him even though she was planning to marry another man.

'I'll tell you later about the malpractice suit,' he said. 'How about that dinner I keep asking you to?'

'When?'

'Tonight?'

She nodded.

'Pick you up at eight,' he said, and walked out of the canteen.

She was on the phone to her mother within minutes. 'Can you babysit for me tonight, Mum?' she asked.

'Of course I can, love,' said her mother. 'Are you going out with Patrick?'

'No, not with Patrick.'

'One of the girls at the hospital, then?' her mother enquired.

Helen couldn't bring herself to admit who her date was, knowing that her mother would strongly disapprove.

'I'll tell you all about it later,' she said.

By the time she'd fed and bathed Robert and settled him in his cot, Helen was feeling the strain of the working day pressing down on her.

She decided to treat herself to a relaxing bath. Pouring in the contents of a small bottle of aromatherapy liquid—a Christmas gift from an aunt—she slid under the delicious-smelling bubbles and enjoyed the very pleasant sensation of pampering herself in the bath's restorative warmth.

With her hair freshly washed and her skin tingling with scented cleanliness, she set about deciding what to wear for her dinner date with Andrew. She agonised over whether to wear a skirt or trousers or, as it was a warm evening, a dress. In the end she settled on what she considered was a smart but casual look— a round-necked black three-quarter sleeve dress and a black-and-grey summer jacket, both of which she'd recently bought in the sales at bargain prices. She looked good, she decided, her weariness and tension having floated away down the plughole with the bath water.

When Andrew arrived she was already waiting at the door, having decided it would not be a good idea for him to meet up with her mother. Dorothy, as Helen had predicted, had expressed great disapproval of her going out with Andrew, muttering ominously, 'I hope you know what you're doing!'

They drove out of the city, heading northeast up into the moorland that could be seen on a clear day from the centre of Milchester.

'I've been recommended a great little place for us to go to tonight,' he said. 'It's in the hills with lovely views. And the food's pretty good, too.'

'Who recommended it to you?' asked Helen for no particular reason. She just wanted to chat at this stage in the evening about unimportant things.

'One of the theatre sisters was telling me about it,' he replied. 'That attractive redhead, Margie Whittaker. Do you remember meeting her at the dance?'

Helen remembered meeting her. She also remembered the way Patrick hadn't been able to keep his eyes off the woman!

'Yes,' said Helen. 'I remember Margie.'

Half an hour later they arrived, and she had to admit that Margie's taste in pubs couldn't be faulted. It had formerly been an old coaching inn and was in the most idyllic setting, with fine views across a large reservoir. Inside was a cheery bar and three very snug oak-beamed rooms divided by thick stone walls.

They selected a table near one of the bow windows which had a magnificent view of the wooded reservoir with the hills behind it and the setting sun streaking blood-red across the water.

Helen was suddenly transported back to her childhood.

'I remember coming here once before,' she said, the view bringing back the past in a flood of memory. 'I'd been hillwalking with my father and we called in here for refreshments. He always planned our walks to include a pub with his favourite beer.' Helen smiled at the recollection, but there was a tinge of sadness in her voice.

'You spent a lot of leisure time with your father, didn't you?' remarked Andrew. 'I envy you that. My father always seemed so wrapped up in his work, so conscientious about everything. He barely had time for family life at all.'

He reached out and touched her hand, entwining her fingers in his. It was a comforting gesture but Helen realised she mustn't read too much into it. They sat in companionable silence as they waited for their meal to arrive, gazing out of the window at the glorious view and the sunset. She'd forgotten how easy he was to be with. She'd been secretly worried that, after all the harsh words that had passed between them, they would have nothing to talk about that wasn't going to be contentious. She was wrong. The time passed extremely pleasantly and before she knew it she was looking at the menu again, wondering if she had room for pudding.

'I'll just have coffee,' she said eventually.

'The same for me,' Andrew told the waiter.

When they were left on their own, Andrew broached the subject that had been on both their minds.

'Chicago,' he said. 'Would you like me to tell you what happened?'

Helen nodded.

Andrew started. 'I was working as an orthopaedic surgeon in a specialist hospital in the city,' he said, folding his hands together and leaning on the table. 'We used to get a lot of sports people coming to us with injuries, knees in particular—ACLs and patella injuries.'

'Your speciality,' added Helen.

'Indeed. One of the patients on whom I operated had the usual ACL injury but unusually it was in both knees. I told the patient, who insisted on having both knees done at the same time, that rest was vital in order that the repair should be successful.'

'Of course,' agreed Helen, stirring milk into her coffee.

'However,' said Andrew, 'the patient didn't do as I'd instructed and as a result the operation wasn't a success. I was sued for negligence to the tune of several million dollars.'

'Good grief!' she exclaimed. 'I realise American courts award massive sums in damages but, even so, I would have thought that was a bit steep.'

'The patient claimed that a very promising golfing career had been ruined. The claim took into account all the winnings that would have accumulated over the next few years.'

'And would the patient have made a top professional golfer, do you think?'

Andrew gave a hollow laugh and shook his head. 'I very much doubt it. I was operating on a very mediocre player, I later discovered, one who had no chance of winning a title at club level let alone on the professional golf circuit.'

'Was it very stressful for you?' asked Helen, adding,

marry. 'He's very easygoing,' she replied. 'And very understanding.'

'Sounds like Mr Wonderful,' said Andrew.

Was he being sarcastic? She couldn't tell.

She decided to take his remark at face value. 'Yes, he is pretty wonderful,' she said.

'In that case, there was something else I wanted to mention to you,' he said. 'How do you fancy a trip to Norfolk? Do you think Patrick will be easygoing about that as well?'

'Norfolk?' she asked in surprise.

'Do you remember me telling you that I owned a house down there?'

'Oh, yes,' she said, recalling a much earlier conversation. 'In the village where you grew up. And I told you that I used to go sailing on the Broads with my father.'

She sighed at the memory. 'I love Norfolk.'

'That's what I thought. Before I leave for the States, I'm planning on going down to sort out what I'm going to do with the house. I wondered if you'd like to come along for a couple of days?'

Helen hesitated. Did she really want to spend a couple of days alone with him? The answer was a definite yes, but she also knew she would weaken and they'd probably end up in bed together again…just like Seattle. And what would that achieve? Only further heartache when he flitted off back to America.

It was as if he'd read her thoughts. 'You needn't worry about my behaviour, if that's what's on your mind. I shall act like a perfect gentleman. I have no intention of trying to seduce a woman who's in love with another man.'

'Not like at the dance, then?'

'Not like at the dance. That night, I was convinced you didn't love Patrick. I now accept that you probably do.' He shrugged his shoulders. 'You win some, you lose some!'

He said it flippantly but it hurt him, nevertheless. Hurt him to admit that Helen didn't love him, she loved Patrick. The more he saw her, the more he wanted her. She'd become a part of him—it was as if she acted as a major artery to his heart. But he now accepted that some things were never meant to be—and, barring a miracle, that seemed to be the case with him and Helen. But he was hopeful she'd come to Norfolk with him. It would be torture having her under the same roof and not touching her! However, he was an honourable man and intended to keep his word.

Helen was desperately keen to go, but there was Robert to consider.

'I'd like to come, of course,' she said. 'But I can't really leave the baby with my mother for two whole days…'

'Bring him along. You did say that I could see him whenever I wanted,' said Andrew, grinning. 'Well, I want to take him to Norfolk to show him his ancestral home!'

CHAPTER TEN

THEY set off early as it was a long drive from Milchester to Norfolk. The car boot was packed to overflowing with baby equipment and supplies, leaving space for little else.

'It's the first time I've taken him anywhere overnight,' said Helen as she squeezed in yet another pack of disposable nappies between the portable cot and the folding buggy.

'Mustn't forget these,' she said, pointing to the two doctors' bags and their own overnight cases.

'No room in the boot,' said Andrew, placing them in the back of the car. 'Now, you keep your eye on these,' he said to Robert, who gurgled back at him.

'Do you know,' said Andrew settling himself into the driver's seat, 'I swear that child understands every word I say?'

Helen fastened her seat belt. 'If he does, it's more than I do!' she said, grinning widely.

Starting up the engine, he grinned back at her. 'I think the breakdowns in communication have been on both sides, Dr Blackburn. But we won't risk spoiling our little excursion by dwelling on that now.'

They stopped on the way for a picnic lunch and Helen fed and changed Robert. He then went to sleep as they continued their journey. After another hour's driving the landscape changed and they were greeted by the distinctive Norfolk sight of summer fields ablaze with poppies.

'I remember it so well!' exclaimed Helen. 'Dad and I used to come sailing here every summer—and although it's years since I've been, it hasn't changed a bit.'

'It is a beautiful part of the country,' said Andrew. 'A beautiful part of the world. I'm glad you like it, too.'

They drove into a particularly scenic village with a large green surrounded by pretty houses and cottages.

'Here we are,' he said, driving past a stone church and turning down a small lane.

'Your house is in this village?' asked Helen.

'That's right,' said Andrew. 'Pretty, isn't it?'

'It's absolutely heavenly,' she said as he pulled up outside an attractive stone and flint house.

'It may look heavenly,' said Andrew grimly, 'but as far as my father was concerned it was a living hell.'

'Not the house, surely? Not this lovely house in this idyllic village?'

'The house was fine,' said Andrew, 'but it was where he was living when all hell broke loose when he was falsely accused of misconduct. Instead of having the confidence to confront it head on, he just gave up and let the strain of it get to him. He was a virtual prisoner in the house, not daring to step outside in case people were talking about him or pointing at him.'

'Is that why you want to sell it, because it has such bad memories for you?'

'Partly. And I just wonder how much time I'll be able to spend here in the future.'

Andrew got out of the car and went around to her side, helping her out.

Robert had started to stir. Helen picked him up and they walked up the small path to the house.

'Is it all shut up?' asked Helen, peering through one of the windows. She noticed dust-sheets over some of the furniture but apart from that it looked as if it was still lived in.

'An elderly aunt who lives in the village keeps an eye on it for me. And a gardener comes once a week to mow the grass and tidy the flower-beds and that kind of thing.'

He opened the front door and stepped inside. 'Just checking there are no burglars or squatters,' he said, before beckoning her in.

They walked through into the kitchen, a lovely sunny room overlooking a pleasant little garden. On the table were a couple of supermarket bags and a note. Andrew picked it up and read it.

'Good old Auntie,' he said. 'I told her we were coming up and she's left everything ready for us. Food in the bags and in the fridge and the beds have been aired.'

Helen walked around the house, holding Robert as she looked in each room.

'This is where your daddy grew up,' she told him, feeling as if she'd stepped back in time.

Andrew came up the stairs with their bags. He put her bag and Robert's cot in one room and his own bag in another.

'Cup of tea?' he asked when they were downstairs again.

'Yes, please,' said Helen. 'And then I'll give Robert his bottle.'

'May I do that?' Andrew asked as he filled up the kettle with cold water from the tap.

'What?'

'Feed Robert. I've never given a baby a bottle before, but I've seen it done on television!' he joked.

Helen made up the milk formula and handed the bottle to Andrew who was holding Robert on his knee. 'You just have to make sure the milk fills the teat. Otherwise he'll take in lots of air and give himself a tummyache.'

She sat down opposite them and drank her tea. It was a moment she'd treasure, she told herself, watching Andrew feed his son. This was going to be a very special couple of days when, for possibly the only time in their lives, they would be like a real family…just the three of them under one roof, playing house.

Later, when Robert had settled down after his feed, they put him in his buggy and pushed him out for a little walk in the sultry evening air.

'Would you mind if we called in on my aunt some time?' asked Andrew. 'I phoned her yesterday and said that we might.'

'Oh, you must,' insisted Helen. 'You wouldn't have come all this way without seeing her, would you?'

Andrew took the handle of the buggy from Helen. 'Of course *I* would be calling in to see her. I just didn't know if you wanted to get involved in the visit as well.'

'I'd love to meet her,' said Helen sincerely. 'What's her name?'

'Isabel,' said Andrew. 'She's my father's sister and a leading light in the local church. I thought we'd call in now as she doesn't live far away.'

'Great,' said Helen.

'There's only one thing,' said Andrew cautiously. 'Can we pretend that we're married? You see, Auntie Isabel is very religious and wouldn't approve of this.' He waved his arms to take in all three of them.

'Oh,' said Helen in surprise. 'So, what will you say? How will you introduce me?'

'I won't make a big thing of introductions,' said Andrew. 'In fact, I've already told her about you and Robert and she just jumped to the conclusion that we were married.'

'But I'm not wearing a ring,' said Helen. 'Won't she notice that?'

'Just tell her you're the modern type who doesn't believe in wearing wedding rings.' He cast her a roguish look. 'Anyway, she'll be so taken up with seeing her great-nephew that she probably won't even notice a minor detail like a missing ring.'

His aunt's house was one of a row of terraced stone cottages on the edge of the village green close to the church. Her small front garden was a blaze of colour, with roses round the door and hollyhocks standing in a tall, colourful row at either side. Clumps of sweet-smelling lavender lined the neat path to the front door.

Isabel had seen them arrive and was standing in the open doorway to greet them. She was a tiny woman but she was bustling with energy and life. Helen took to her immediately.

'You must be Helen,' she said, clasping her by the hand. Peering into the buggy, she exclaimed, 'He's just like his daddy, isn't he? What a little sweetie. And how lovely that you named him Robert after his grandfather. My brother would have been so delighted!' she babbled on.

'Would you like to hold him?' Helen offered.

'Yes, please. I don't think I've held a baby since Andrew was tiny, but you don't lose the knack, do you?'

Helen placed Robert in her arms and she rocked him gently, almost reverently.

'Do you have children of your own?' Helen asked.

'Good heavens, no!' said Isabel. 'I'm not married, never have been. I'm an old maid and proud of it!' She continued to rock the baby, cooing at him. 'I know people have a different attitude nowadays, but in my time we didn't approve of single women having children.' She handed Robert back to Helen. 'I wouldn't have countenanced it myself. I don't approve of that kind of loose behaviour. And now, my dears, do come in. I've opened a bottle of my special home-made elderberry wine for the occasion.'

Later that evening, when Robert had been bathed and put to bed, Andrew drove to the nearest take-away for their evening meal.

'Two large portions of fish, chips and mushy peas,' he announced as he walked into the house with his purchase.

'Ooh, that smells so good,' enthused Helen, who

was cutting the crusty loaf that Isabel had left for them. She brought out the warmed plates from the oven and Andrew opened a bottle of chilled white wine.

'A feast fit for a king,' he exclaimed as they tucked in with relish.

'I hadn't realised how hungry I'd got,' said Helen, as she speared another forkful of the tasty battered cod.

'I always find that happens to me in Norfolk,' said Andrew. 'The east coast air is very bracing, as they used to say in the holiday posters.'

They finished their meal with fresh peaches and nectarines and a selection of cheeses, which they ate with the remainder of the crusty bread.

'I must say your aunt has impeccable taste when it comes to buying food. The cheeses and the bread are wonderful.'

'She makes her own bread,' said Andrew. 'That's why it tastes so good. But I drew the line at the wine, insisting on bringing my own choice rather than take up her offer of a bottle of that home-made stuff.'

'It wasn't too bad,' said Helen gallantly. 'I think she's a lovely lady. Was she very attractive in her younger days?'

'My father used to say she was,' replied Andrew, pouring them another glass of wine. 'He also said that his sister was far too fussy about men and that's why she could never find one to suit her.'

Helen sipped her wine reflectively. Being fussy must run in the family, she decided…not being able to commit to one person in case something better, or someone better, comes along.

When they'd finished their meal, cleared the table and done the washing-up, Helen stifled a yawn.

'I'm sorry,' she said, 'I just can't keep my eyes open. I suppose I can blame that on the bracing Norfolk air, too!'

'It's been a long day,' said Andrew. 'We had a very early start. I'm ready for bed myself. I think I'll walk outside for a little while before turning in.' He kissed her on the cheek. 'You go up now and I'll lock up when I come in.'

He walked out of the kitchen and strode through the hall and out of the front door, closing it softly behind him so that he wouldn't wake the baby.

The next day they set off after breakfast to spend the morning on the Norfolk coast before driving back to Milchester.

They parked the car in the car park of a pub where they planned to have lunch after they'd spent some time walking round the small seaside resort. They pushed Robert's buggy along the narrow, medieval streets to the seafront and the sheltered beach where the cliffs rose steeply at either side.

Back at the pub they settled down at a corner table where they could find room for Robert's baby chair. They ordered sandwiches and soft drinks.

While she was waiting for them to arrive, Helen went to the ladies' to wash her hands. On the way back she found herself behind a man and woman and two boys, one of whom was in a wheelchair. The other boy, Helen noticed, was limping. As they went up to the bar, Helen overheard the man say, 'Come on, Ben, stop putting it on. There's absolutely nothing the matter with your leg and you know it!'

'There is, Dad!' protested the boy. 'I can't help it!'

Helen made her way back to her table and sat down. She pointed out the boy and his father to Andrew.

'That child's limping quite badly,' she said. 'His father seems to think he's making it up.'

Andrew shrugged. 'Kids do, you know. Perhaps he wants to get out of school tomorrow.'

They started to eat their sandwiches, and within a short time the parents and the two boys had seated themselves nearby, the boy and his wheelchair fitting into a space next to the pub table.

'Here you are, Simon,' the woman said to the boy in the wheelchair. 'Your favourite crisps. I'll put your drink here and you can reach it yourself.'

'Can Ben have some of my crisps?' asked Simon.

'No, he can't,' answered the father. 'You know he's in training.'

Helen and Andrew couldn't help overhearing the conversation as they were the only other people in the pub alcove. They looked at each other and silently raised their eyebrows. Helen mouthed, 'Training for what? He's only a kid.'

'How's your leg, Ben?' his mother asked. 'Is it still hurting?'

Before the boy could answer, his father butted in. 'There's nothing wrong with him, I keep telling you. He's just trying to get out of his sports training because we're on holiday.'

Helen noticed the boy's face. It was hard to tell whether or not he was making up the story. But she was touched to see that Simon looked at Ben with a big smile and winked at him. This gesture of solidarity appeared to cheer up the other boy who smiled back. The boys looked very alike—they were probably brothers, she decided.

'Does it really hurt?' Simon asked in a low voice.

'It's all right. It's not too bad, anyway,' replied Ben.

Helen found herself becoming increasingly interested in the family and in particular the two boys. She was puzzled by the situation and moved by the concern the brothers seemed to have for each other.

Her eyes moved down to Ben's legs, the subject of the family discussion. He was wearing running shorts and Helen thought she could detect, even from where she was sitting, that one knee appeared different from the other. She thought she could see a swelling on the left shin just below the knee.

The boy stood up to let his father get past him and in doing so stumbled and almost fell against Robert's baby chair.

'Sorry,' he said, limping back to his own seat.

'That's all right,' said Helen. 'But are *you* all right yourself? You seem to be having a bit of a problem with your leg.'

The boy's eyes darted to his father before answering.

'I'm fine,' he said. 'My dad says so.'

When the father was away at the bar, Helen caught the mother's eye. Noticing that Ben was rubbing his leg, a pained expression on his face, she decided to say something.

'Is your son really OK?' she asked. 'Or does he have some sort of injury?'

'I'm not really sure,' said the mother, keeping her voice low and conspiratorial. 'My husband seems to think Ben's making it up, but the leg looks a bit swollen to me.'

'Would you like me to have a look at it?' Helen asked. 'I specialise in sports injuries and I might be able to tell if it's necessary for you to take him to see his own doctor.'

The woman was undecided, casting a surreptitious look at where her husband was.

'I think you should look at my brother's knee,' Simon piped up. 'Dad thinks he's making it up but I know my brother wouldn't do that. Please, would you see if there's anything wrong with him?'

Helen and the woman exchanged glances. The woman said, 'Yes, I would be grateful if you could tell us if there's anything we should be worried about. Ben has such a rigorous training programme and I often wonder if that's half the problem.'

Helen slid out of the bench seat, saying to Andrew, 'I'll take a look first and, if necessary, will you give a second opinion?' He nodded in agreement. Like Helen, he was beginning to be concerned about the boy and whether he'd injured himself in training.

She went over to where Ben was sitting.

'My name's Helen,' she said. 'I'm a doctor. How old are you, Ben?'

'Eleven,' he replied.

The boy was small for his age, she judged. No doubt he'd catch up once he'd had his growth spurt.

'Can you stand up for a moment so I can compare

one leg with the other?' she asked. As she looked at his legs she could see at once that there was a marked difference in appearance between the two. His left leg had a significant swelling below the knee. As she touched it gently he flinched.

'Does that hurt?'

'A little,' he said, biting his lip and trying to be brave. It was obvious to Helen that it hurt more than a little. She noticed the way Ben's eyes darted across to his father who was now walking back from the bar, carrying drinks.

'What's going on here?' he asked, seeing Helen placing her hands on Ben's knees.

'This lady is having a look at Ben's knee,' said his mother. 'She specialises in sports injuries.'

'I keep telling you,' he protested to her, 'Ben's making it up! There's nothing wrong with his leg.'

'I think there may be a problem,' Helen said quietly.

'And are you a doctor or something? Or just a crackpot?' The man laughed unpleasantly.

'I'm a doctor,' she said squaring up to the man. 'Dr Helen Blackburn.'

'And a very good one,' said Andrew from the corner of the room.

'And what do *you* know about it?' asked the man, surprised at Andrew's intervention.

'I'm also a doctor,' he replied.

'Blimey,' said the man, 'what *is* this, a doctors' convention?'

'Just let Dr Blackburn get on with her examination,' said Ben's mother assertively in a voice that meant business.

Helen continued her dialogue with the boy.

'Do you do a lot of sport, Ben?' she asked.

'I do a lot of running. It's part of my sports training regime,' he replied, as if quoting someone else. Helen had a suspicion that he was using his father's words. This was confirmed when the father intervened.

'You need to start young these days if you're going to excel at sport. Ben's very good at football and we're hoping he'll catch the eye of a talent scout from one of the top football clubs. They spot 'em young these days. A local boy, twelve years old, was signed up last month.'

Helen made a mental note—ambitious parent, possibly pushing child too fast.

'You said you did a lot of running, Ben. How much do you do?'

'Four miles,' he replied.

'Every week?'

'Every day. Sometimes before I go to school, sometimes after.'

'Where exactly is the pain?' Helen asked.

'Here and here,' he said pointing to areas above and below the knee.

'Is it bad all the time or just during sport?'

'It hurts a bit when I'm walking, but mostly it's when I'm running.'

His father gave a snort. 'That's his excuse for not keeping up with his sports training regime.'

'Oh, Dad!' said Ben.

Helen carried on examining the boy's knee, convinced of her diagnosis and equally convinced that his father wasn't going to be at all happy with what she was about to say. She stood up and faced the man.

'I believe that Ben may have a condition called osteochondritis, which affects the bones of some children as they are growing. It's known as Osgood-Schlatter disease and it affects the knee.'

'Oh, no!' said his mother looking stricken. 'How did he get that?'

'It's caused by repeated exercise and it's most common in children, usually boys, aged between ten and fourteen,' Helen replied.

'Osgood what?' exclaimed the father. 'I've never heard of it! Is it catching?'

'No, it's not infectious,' assured Helen. 'It happens as a result of repeated pulling of the muscle at the front of the thigh on the tendon which is attached to the shin. It creates pain above and below the knee and a swelling like this.' She gently touched Ben's leg. 'It gets worse during strenuous activity like running or other vigorous sport.'

'So he's not making it up!' said his father. Helen noticed he'd gone quite red in the face. Whether the man was blushing with shame or just plain angry she couldn't tell.

'I wouldn't make it up, Dad!' protested Ben.

'Is my brother going to be all right?' asked Simon anxiously. 'He was running for me…because I can't run or play football…and now I feel it's all my fault!'

'Of course it's not your fault,' said his mother. 'If it's anyone's fault, it's his!' She pointed an accusing finger at her husband who went an even deeper shade of red. 'Nagging the boy to do his sports training all the time.'

'No, Mum,' said Ben. 'Dad didn't force me. I

wanted to do it. I want to keep on running…I want to become a famous footballer!'

'I'm afraid you'll have to slow down your sports training regime for the time being, Ben,' said Helen gently. 'In fact, you'll have to stop it completely for a while until the swelling goes down and the pain disappears.'

The boy looked downcast. 'If I go to my doctor, will he give me some of those pills or injections that they give to injured footballers so they can keep on playing?'

'No,' said Helen and his parents in unison. Helen smiled at them both, relieved that the parents seemed to be united in wanting to do the best for their son.

'I'm not going to give you anything except advice,' said Helen, 'and I predict that your own doctor will feel the same. Osgood-Schlatter's often clears up completely without any treatment at all, apart from rest. Rest is vital, Ben, in order to prevent deformity. It's something you'll grow out of eventually and then you can take up your sports training again, although I'd advise a less vigorous regime in future. Swimming is very good for physical training, you know. And it might be better for you than all that running.'

'Yeah,' said Simon enthusiastically. 'I can watch you at the pool-side and time the lengths!'

'Good idea,' said Helen. 'But not yet. Your brother has to rest that leg of his. Will you make sure he does?'

'You bet!' said Simon, picking up the crisp packet. 'Here you are, Ben. You can have some of these now that you're not in training.'

Helen returned to her own table.

Andrew touched her arm. 'You handled that well,' he said in a low voice. 'Could have been a bit tricky with the father breathing down your neck.'

'I've been thinking,' she said as she sat down next to him. 'I might suggest to the hospital that we start up a junior sports injuries clinic. We could publicise it through the education department and involve the local schools.'

'It's a good idea but you may have to be realistic—these things cost a lot of money,' said Andrew. 'Don't you remember in America how they had all kinds of outside funding for those types of specialist units?'

'I was just thinking out loud,' said Helen, pondering the issue. 'I don't see why the hospital shouldn't approach somewhere like Milchester United for funding. A major football club like that would probably be happy to cough up some funds. After all, they have junior teams themselves and their talent scouts are constantly on the lookout for youngsters like Ben. It could be great,' she went on, letting her enthusiasm carry her away. 'I can see it now—the Milchester United Junior Sports Injuries Clinic!'

'And, no doubt, you'll be in charge of it,' said Andrew.

'Of course. You're not the only one who's ambitious, you know!'

Andrew stiffened defensively. 'What do you mean, ambitious?'

She laughed. 'Oh, you know, wanting to get on, wanting to be a success…'

He wasn't smiling. 'I know what ambitious means! I mean, why me in particular and why mention it now?'

'Well, you're going back to America to take up that post, aren't you? That's what I meant by ambitious.'

'I signed the American contract before I knew I had a son over here. I'll be coming back to England as soon as I realistically can in order to be near him.'

Oh, yes, his son! No mention of me, Helen noted. Maybe he'll also be bringing his American lover back with him!

She bent down and picked up the soft toy that Robert had dropped. She mustn't dwell too closely on the future…just enjoy what they had now because the last thing she wanted on this blissful weekend was to have an argument with him. There was precious little time left for them to play Happy Families and she was determined to wave him off to America with only good memories of their time together. There would be time enough to be unhappy once he'd gone back to Chicago and his lover.

Andrew checked his watch. 'Time we were making a move.'

They were walking back to their car and Andrew was carrying Robert when someone called out to them. They looked to see who it was and saw Ben's mother running across the car park towards them.

'Excuse me,' she said. 'I think you dropped this inside the pub.' She waved a small rattle in the air and shook it. Robert's face lit up as he heard the noise and he began to gurgle with delight.

'Thank you,' said Helen, accepting the rattle.

'He's a lovely baby,' said the woman. 'He looks just like you,' she told Andrew, who was still holding his son. 'He's very bonny.'

She stroked Robert's chubby little legs. 'Simon was

a very bonny baby,' she said wistfully. 'It was such a tragedy when he was born with spina bifida…but he's a plucky kid and we all love him so much. Particularly Ben.'

'I could tell that the boys were very fond of each other,' said Helen. 'That's not always the case with siblings!'

She noticed the way the woman was looking longingly at Robert, perhaps recalling her own children when they were small.

'It must have been hard for you, having a child with spina bifida,' said Helen, sensing that the woman wanted to talk about it.

She nodded. 'But somehow it was harder for my husband. He took it very badly. He's always been a mad keen sportsman and imagined running around the playing fields, kicking a football with his first-born son. He talked of nothing else during my pregnancy. Even saying things like. ''If it's a girl we're going to keep on trying until we get a boy''! Imagine how he felt when the baby was, after all, the longed-for son but one who would spend his life in a wheelchair.'

'Is that why he's so ambitious for Ben?' asked Andrew.

'I think so,' she said. 'But it wasn't one-sided— Ben was also very keen. I don't think my husband forced him to do anything against his will. I'd have made sure about that…and so would Simon.'

'You'll be taking Ben to see your own doctor, won't you?' Helen asked.

'As soon as we get home,' said the woman. 'I just wanted to say thank you to you two doctors for warning us about the condition.'

'How will your husband take it?' Andrew asked.

'He'll be fine,' she said. 'I can assure you that the last thing he wants is to end up with two children in wheelchairs.'

CHAPTER ELEVEN

A WEEK later, Helen was at home and it was break-fast-time.

'Any post for me?' she asked as she placed Robert in his baby seat. 'I thought I heard the postman come a few minutes ago.'

Jack handed her a couple of envelopes as he sorted through the morning's mail.

Her mother watched Helen as she took the letters and put them on one side.

'Not opening them?' she said quizzically. 'I can never wait for more than a couple of seconds before opening my letters even though I know most of them are going to be bills!'

'I'll open them later,' said Helen evasively.

'Suit yourself,' said Dorothy, who was obviously dying to know what was inside the envelopes. 'Would you like a cup of tea? I bought your favourite—cam-omile and spearmint—when I was out shopping yes-terday.'

'Yes, please,' said Helen, who continued to attend to Robert, leaving the unopened letters on the table.

When her mother handed her the mug of tea, it amused Helen to see that her eyes were fixed on the mysterious letters…mysterious, that was, to her mother.

'All right, Mum, you win!' Helen picked them up

and tore open the envelopes. 'See, a credit-card bill,' she said, waving it in front of her mother.

She pulled out the contents of the larger envelope more gingerly, trying to play down what was inside. 'And here are some house details, that's all.'

'House details? That's nice. Is it for you and Patrick? Oh, do let me see!'

Before Helen could reply, Dorothy had leaned over and taken the estate agent's printed pages.

There were several sheets and Dorothy glanced at each one quickly, a disappointed look crossing her face.

'But these are only houses for renting,' she said, 'and they're very small, and not in a very good area either.'

Helen reached over and took the house details from her mother.

'It's all I can afford,' she said quickly, annoyed that she'd been caught out in this way. She had been hoping to get herself fixed up with her own place before having to announce it to her parents. As it was, they both were staring at her with questioning looks on their faces and she knew she'd have to start explaining.

She decided to cause a diversion, taking the spotlight away from herself and her future plans. She faced her stepfather who'd been reading the morning paper.

'Shouldn't you be in the office by now, Jack?' she said, gesturing to her watch.

'I'm not going in today,' he said. 'I've brought some work home. I need a bit of peace and quiet to read through some papers and—'

'Never mind that,' interrupted Dorothy. 'What's all this about Helen wanting to rent a terraced house? What does Patrick think about it? I'm amazed that he can't come up with anything better for the two of you in which to start your married life.'

'We're not getting married,' said Helen. 'We called it off yesterday—and then I rang round the estate agents, asking them to send me particulars of small houses that would be suitable for me and Robert.'

'I knew it!' said her mother. 'It's all Andrew's fault! I warned you that you shouldn't have gone away with him. Patrick must have been terribly upset. I suggest you apologise and try and make it up with him.'

'No, Mum. It wasn't anything to do with the week-end in Norfolk. Patrick had no qualms about that. I broke off the engagement because the marriage would never have worked.'

'Why not?' Her mother was shocked. 'He's such a nice man and he's so fond of you, Helen.'

'But that's not enough, is it?' Helen replied sadly. 'I can't marry someone I don't love. And I don't love Patrick.'

'What does Patrick say about it?' asked Jack.

Helen took a sip of tea before replying, hoping that the camomile would have a calming effect on her.

'He was very understanding—as he always is. And actually I don't think it came as a huge surprise to him. We'll always be friends, but never lovers.'

Jack put down his newspaper. 'If the spark isn't there, it isn't there. It's all a matter of chemistry.'

Her mother wasn't so easily placated. 'But you

both get on so well. And little Robert needs a father—'

'She doesn't love him, Dorothy,' said Jack firmly, 'and that's all there is to it!'

Her mother frowned. 'So why are you looking at house particulars? There's no need for you to move out of here. I've told Jack we're not moving anywhere until the time is right for you.'

Helen could sense her mother's embarrassment. On the one hand she wanted to please Jack and plan for his retirement—on the other hand she was desperately keen not to appear as if she was pushing her daughter and grandson out onto the street!

Helen patted her mother's hand. 'I'm moving out because I want a place of my own. It's got nothing to do with you and Jack.'

'You can't afford it, love. Not on what you earn part time. It doesn't take a mathematical genius to work that out.'

'I've worked it all out, don't worry,' said Helen brightly. 'I've applied for a full-time position at the hospital, in the orthopaedic outpatients department. It's virtually a nine-to-five job, so I can place Robert with a childminder on the days you can't have him.'

'You know you can stay here,' said her mother.

'Mum,' said Helen softly, 'no disrespect to you and Jack, but I need to have my own space. I need to feel that I'm independent.'

'We understand that,' said Jack briskly, getting up from the breakfast table. 'Now, if you ladies will excuse me, I'm going to my study to get on with some work.' He winked surreptitiously at Helen as he went out, mouthing the words, 'Good luck'.

*   *   *

Another week passed. Helen's afternoon shift at the open access clinic had finished and she picked up her bag and headed for the door at top speed.

'You're in a hurry,' said the desk nurse. Normally Helen would stop for a chat before leaving for home.

'I want to catch someone before I go,' she said in explanation, walking quickly towards the orthopaedic department. She had something to give to Andrew—a photograph of Robert—and she was looking forward to seeing his reaction to the picture. When Andrew had dropped them back home after their Norfolk trip a couple of weeks previously, he'd asked her for a photo of the baby. 'I don't have a camera,' he confessed, 'but I'd love a picture of him to take with me when I leave Milchester.'

Helen had, as it so happened, a new photograph of Robert, taken by Jack with his state-of-the-art digital camera, and it was excellent. She'd had a large print made for Andrew. On the back she'd attached a piece of paper with Robert's details written on it—things like his date of birth, how much he'd weighed at birth and how much he weighed now…the kind of details that Andrew most likely didn't know and yet would, she hoped, find interesting.

As she walked into his department she was disappointed to see that his door was shut, indicating perhaps that he was seeing a patient.

'Do you think Dr Henderson will be busy for long?' she asked the desk nurse. 'I have to get home soon and I was hoping to catch him before I leave.'

'He's finished his appointments,' she said. 'He's

just got a friend in there, I think. I'll just buzz him for you.'

She pressed the intercom button. 'Dr Blackburn would like to see you for a moment,' she said.

'Tell her to come in,' Andrew replied.

The nurse smiled at Helen and waved her arm in the direction of Andrew's consulting room. 'You heard what the man said!'

Helen opened the door gingerly, feeling slightly guilty at her intrusion—but on seeing her Andrew immediately put her at her ease.

'Come in, Helen,' he said giving her one of his devastating smiles. Sitting across from him was a young woman in her twenties. 'Meet Jill Martin,' said Andrew. 'Jill, this is a colleague of mine, Dr Helen Blackburn.'

'Hi, there, Helen,' said Jill. 'It's good to meet you.'

Helen was somewhat surprised to note that Jill had an American accent.

'Nice to meet you, too,' she replied. Then, feeling that she was, after all, intruding on a private meeting, she handed Andrew a buff hard-backed envelope.

'Here's the picture you asked for,' she said. 'The one of Robert.'

She turned to leave but Andrew called her back. 'Don't go,' he said opening the envelope and taking out the photograph. 'It's a great picture,' he said.

'Nice baby,' said Jill, admiring the photograph which Andrew was now showing to her. 'Whose is it?'

'Mine,' said Andrew quickly and with pride. 'He's my son.'

'Wow!' said Jill. 'You certainly kept *him* under

your hat. I wonder what Mom would have to say about that! He's gorgeous, Andrew!'

'I'd better explain who Jill is,' said Andrew to Helen. 'She's the daughter of Lori Martin, someone I know in Chicago, and she's working in London for a month on a student work exchange programme.'

Helen felt the blood drain from her face. 'Lori Martin's daughter?' she said incredulously.

'That's right,' said Jill brightly. 'Do you know Mom?'

'No,' said Helen through clenched teeth.

'It was just the way you said her name—I thought you might know her.'

Helen shook her head wordlessly. She knew the name all right. She'd seen the pictures. She'd heard the voice. She'd drawn the conclusions.

Jill babbled on happily. 'When I got this work exchange Mom said that I was to come up to Milchester and persuade Andrew to come back to the States. And now he tells me that he is coming back, but only for a short time!' She turned to Andrew. 'You're really needed over there, you know. Tell him, Helen. Tell him he's got to stay in America for a long, long time!'

Helen began to feel light-headed. The last person she'd imagined she'd ever find sitting in Andrew's consulting room had been Lori Martin's daughter! She didn't even know such a person had existed, for heaven's sake!

'I hope you don't think I'm rude, but I must be going,' said Helen, edging towards the door. 'Nice to meet you, Jill. See you another time, Andrew.'

She left his room and headed out of the hospital to

the car park. When she got into her car she was shaking so much at first that she didn't trust herself to drive. She turned on the radio and tuned it to a classical station, letting the soothing music flow over her until she felt calmer.

She was particularly upset because she'd been so looking forward to showing Andrew the photo and talking about Robert. Andrew hadn't even noticed the little details she'd written on the back of the picture. She'd also decided to tell Andrew that she and Patrick were no longer getting married—just to see if that made any difference to how he acted towards her. And then, against all expectations, the day had turned into a nightmare as she'd been confronted by his lover's daughter!

The next morning Andrew was half an hour into a hip-replacement operation when he picked up on a conversation between the theatre sister and one of her nurses.

The theatre sister was Margie Whittaker, the statuesque redhead who set many a male colleague's heart racing. Andrew liked her—she was very efficient at her job—but he didn't lust after her in the way that he knew others did. He also tended not to pay much attention to the gossipy chitchat that went on across the operating theatre, preferring to focus his whole mind on the operation.

The nurse who was preparing the instrument tray said to Margie, 'How's your social life these days? I've heard you've got a new man.'

'That's right,' confirmed Margie. 'I've really hit it

off with this guy, even though we've only been on two dates. I think it could be the real thing!'

'So tell me more,' said the nurse. 'What's his name and what does he do?'

'He's called Patrick,' said Margie, 'and he's a doctor, a GP. He's a really sweet man.'

Andrew continued to operate, taking on board this piece of information. He processed it in his mind because he thought it had a familiar ring to it. He thought it might be important to him but he couldn't think why.

After he'd finished the operation and was stripping off his latex gloves it suddenly came to him. Patrick! That was the name of Helen's fiancé. He was a GP and, damn it, he'd been the man Andrew had seen slipping out of the dance that evening with the luscious Margie!

'Margie,' he said, 'this Patrick—is he anything to do with Dr Helen Blackburn?'

'He was,' she said, 'but not any more. She broke off the engagement.'

Andrew was amazed. 'She did? When?'

'About a week ago,' said Margie. 'He was very fond of her, and she had this little boy that he was crazy about, but it just didn't work out. She never loved him because she's in love with someone else, he says. So they've agreed to be just good friends. He realises it's all for the best.'

Andrew was reeling from what he'd just heard. A great weight had lifted from his shoulders. Helen wasn't going to marry Patrick because she'd never loved him! It was the best piece of news he'd heard in a long time. He finished the hip operation with a huge grin on his face. There was hope for him at last!

After he'd completed that morning's list he decided to walk over to the open access unit to see if he could find Helen.

He was disappointed but not surprised to find that Helen wasn't there. He had a sneaking feeling that it was one of the days that she spent at home.

As he walked through a ward he bumped into Dorothy Talbot.

'I was hoping to speak to Helen,' he told her, 'but she isn't at work today. Would you happen to know if she's at home now? I might call round to see her.'

Dorothy had been told about the Jill Martin incident. Helen had arrived home in a distressed state. She'd told the whole story to her mother and had felt a good deal better once she'd got it off her chest. 'Why do I waste my time loving him, Mum?' she said. 'When will I ever learn?' So Dorothy was not best minded to be helpful to Andrew at this particular moment.

'I don't believe you'll find her at home, Dr Henderson,' she said brusquely. 'And I don't believe she'd welcome a visit or a call from you.'

'I'll be the judge of that, Nurse Talbot,' said Andrew pleasantly but firmly, more determined than ever to see Helen—and the sooner the better.

Helen had just managed to get Robert off to sleep after his lunchtime feed.

She was sitting at the kitchen table, relaxing, eating a sandwich and reading the morning paper, when the doorbell rang. She raced to the door before whoever it was rang the bell again and woke Robert up.

'Oh, it's you,' she said on seeing Andrew on the doorstep. 'You'd better come in but don't slam the door behind you. You'll wake the baby.'

He followed her into the kitchen and saw the half-eaten sandwich.

'I'm sorry to interrupt your lunch,' he said.

'You'd better have a good reason,' she replied. 'I was reading a fascinating article entitled ''Why Men Cheat on Women''. I'm rather unsophisticated in these matters, as I'm sure you're aware. I suppose I'm a bit of a trusting fool, especially when it comes to dealing with someone like you!'

Andrew totally ignored her outburst. 'I'll take you up on that offer of a coffee,' he said calmly.

'I didn't offer you a coffee! I only asked you in so we could avoid making a scene on the doorstep.'

'I have no intention of making a scene,' he said, walking over to the kettle and switching it on. 'I've been operating all morning and have come straight here. Hence my need for a coffee before we settle down to a cool, dispassionate discussion about us.'

'There's not a lot to say, is there?' said Helen in exasperation. 'You're always doing this to me, Andrew. Just when I think I've got you out of my system, you turn up and cause havoc with my emotions, with my life.' She waved her arms expansively. 'By all means have your coffee, but as for the discussion about ''us'', leave me out of it!'

He continued as if she hadn't spoken a word, making himself a coffee, bringing it to the table and sitting down facing her. 'I was operating this morning, as I've just said, and I discovered something.'

'You've come here for a medical discussion? You want to talk about an operation?' Helen put the flat of her hand against her forehead in an over-dramatic gesture. 'You never cease to amaze me! It's a consultation he wants!' she said, as if addressing an invisible audience.

Andrew pressed on. 'Margie Whittaker was the theatre sister. She told me that she's dating Patrick. *Your* Patrick.'

Helen took a couple of moments to digest this information.

'That's nice,' she said. 'I'm glad about that.'

'She told me that you'd broken off your engagement,' said Andrew, keeping his fingers crossed under the table.

'Yes.' Helen paused. 'You see, I didn't love him. You were right all along. I hope that makes you feel pleased.'

'It makes me feel very pleased,' admitted Andrew.

Helen narrowed her eyes. 'You mean to tell me you've come round here to gloat?'

'Of course not!'

Helen leaned back in her chair and gazed out of the window into the garden. 'It certainly looks that way to me,' she said. 'And now you've had it confirmed that I can't marry Patrick because…well, you know why, I suppose you can't wait to get back to America to live with this woman in Chicago. The one you've been having an affair with.'

He looked astonished. 'Who? What woman in Chicago?'

Helen banged her empty cup down on the table. 'Lori Martin, that's who! She even sent her daughter over to make sure you came back!'

Andrew threw his head back and roared with laughter. 'You think I'm having an affair with Lori?'

'Well, aren't you?'

'No!' He grinned at her. 'Is that what you thought?'

'Yes! And I might have guessed you'd deny it! Well, I've seen the evidence.'

'What evidence?'

'Those photographs. I saw them on your desk!'

Andrew was puzzled. 'I haven't got any photographs of Lori.'

'Yes, you have! And she'd written all lovy-dovy stuff on the back. ''Happy Memories of Chicago from Lori.'' I saw it with my own eyes.'

'You mean that picture of a woman golfer?' said Andrew, comprehension dawning.

Helen nodded mutely.

'That wasn't Lori,' he said. 'That was the woman who sued me for medical negligence.'

'Woman golfer?' said Helen. 'I thought you'd been sued by a man.'

'No, it was a woman. A lying, cheating rogue of a woman. Lori was the lawyer who defended me.'

Helen's jaw dropped.

'Lori hired a private detective to get material that could be used to back up our case,' explained Andrew. 'The patient had both knees operated on and I'd made it a condition of doing both at the same time that she would rest and refrain from playing golf for many months—until I gave her the all-clear to do so. She signed a form to that effect. Then we discovered a video that proved that the woman had played golf a very short time after the operation. No wonder it failed!'

Helen remained speechless as Andrew explained further how the video uncovered by the detective had been accurately dated because at one point a club-house could be seen in the background. On the roof was a digital clock showing the time, temperature and date. What Helen had seen on Andrew's desk were stills taken from the video and sent to him by Lori.

'The ''Happy Memories'' line was Lori being ironic,' he said. 'The last thing those golfing pictures brought back was happy memories!'

Helen was visibly relieved. 'I was convinced you had a woman in Chicago and that you were possibly waiting for her to get a divorce. I once bumped into Mary Oberon in New York and she said that you were using a lawyer who was associated with her husband's law firm. His practice, she told me, specialised in divorce. I put two and two together and came up with the wrong answer!'

Andrew stood up and walked the couple of steps to her side.

'Perhaps now you'll come up with the right answer.' He raised her to her feet and slipped his arms around her waist. 'Will you marry me, you stupid woman?'

CHAPTER TWELVE

IT WAS New Year's Eve and the ice rink in front of the Rockefeller Center was filled with skaters enjoying the holiday atmosphere and the crisp winter air.

The skaters were being watched by a good-natured crowd of tourists and native New Yorkers who were leaning over the rails and spilling out onto the broad pavement.

Among the crowd of onlookers was a young woman from Iowa who was spending the New Year holiday with friends in the city. She was minding their small child, who was dressed like an Inuit, while they were skating. She lifted him out of his buggy and held him up so that he could see the colourful scene below.

'Look, Robert,' she said, 'there's Mummy and Daddy! Can you see them skating? They're waving to you.'

Jane took the hand of the nine-month-old and waved it for him.

'That's a clever boy,' she said as he began to get the idea and started to wave enthusiastically on his own. 'We're having a great time, aren't we?'

Down among the skaters, Helen and Andrew were also having a great time as they glided hand in hand across the ice in the magical setting of the world's most romantic ice rink.

'You're a really good skater,' said Andrew admiringly.

'I learned as a child at Milchester Ice Palace,' replied Helen.

'I might have known it! Is there any sport you're not brilliant at? Please, tell me there is!'

'I'm no good at golf,' she said, trying hard to concentrate on avoiding bumping into the other skaters.

'In that case, I challenge you to a game,' joked Andrew. He waved again to Robert and Jane. 'Do you think our son and his godmother would object if we did another circuit of the rink? It's pretty cold standing around up there.'

'They're both warmly wrapped up,' said Helen. 'Let's do one more time round and then head back to the apartment for a hot toddy followed by a New Year's Eve celebration meal.'

'New Year's Eve!' said Andrew reflectively. 'I remember saying that I'd bring you here on New Year's Eve—and here we are.'

'I'm not sure at the time that I believed it would happen,' said Helen. 'Now that it has, I still can't quite believe it. In fact, I'm finding it hard to take in everything that's happened in the past few months…getting married, moving from Milchester to New York.'

'Only for a couple of years, and then back home to England,' said Andrew.

The both smiled broadly at each other, a picture of complete happiness.

'It's been an amazingly eventful year all round,' said Andrew. 'It started so badly for me, searching all over for you, not knowing where you were. And by the end of the year I'm the father of a gorgeous little boy and married to the woman of my dreams.'

'That's not how you put it in your proposal!' she said jokingly, as they both stepped off the ice.

'Didn't I?' said Andrew innocently. 'I think you must have misheard me.'

Helen grinned and gently touched his face. 'Idiot,' she said.

Modern Romance™
...seduction and
passion guaranteed

Tender Romance™
...love affairs that
last a lifetime

Sensual Romance™
...sassy, sexy and
seductive

Blaze
...sultry days and
steamy nights

Medical Romance™
...medical drama on
the pulse

Historical Romance™
...rich, vivid and
passionate

27 new titles every month.

*With all kinds of Romance for
every kind of mood...*

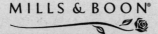

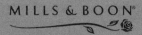

MILLS & BOON®

Medical Romance™

A DOCTOR'S HONOUR *by Jessica Matthews*

Gavin and Aly seemed destined to marry – until Gavin lost the battle to save Aly's cousin. He blamed himself, and felt compelled to leave town and the woman he loved. Three years later Aly found a way for Gavin to return. Her clinic desperately needed a doctor – and she desperately needed to convince Gavin they still had a future!

A FAMILY OF THEIR OWN *by Jennifer Taylor*

Nurse Leanne Russell left Australia in search of her real mother – she found Dr Nick Slater. She's dreamed of a family of her own and now she knows she wants that family with Nick. But Nick has vowed never to marry – it wouldn't be fair to have children. Unless his love for Leanne is enough to persuade him to take a chance…

PARAMEDIC PARTNERS *by Abigail Gordon*

Trainee paramedic Selina Sanderson feels the electricity as soon as she sets eyes on her gorgeous new boss. She soon realises her feelings are deep – but why is he so uncomfortable with a female partner? Kane wants more than anything to be part of Selina's life – but if she discovers the secret he's trying to leave behind she might never trust him again…

On sale 6th September 2002

Available at most branches of WH Smith, Tesco, Martins, Borders, Eason, Sainsbury's and most good paperback bookshops.

0802/03a

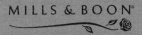

Medical Romance™

A DOCTOR'S COURAGE *by Gill Sanderson*

The new GP in her country practice is unlike any man District Nurse Nikki Gale has met before. The more she gets to know Dr Tom Murray, the more she wants him. Tom's prognosis for the future is uncertain, but Nikki is determined to show him he doesn't have to face his fears alone.

THE NURSE'S SECRET CHILD *by Sheila Danton*

Though Max and Jenny had a passionate relationship, marriage and children had never featured in their future plans. Only Jenny became pregnant — and before she could tell Max she discovered he had always intended to marry someone else. Four years on, Max is back — as a consultant in her hospital! And now she has to decide how to tell Max about her secret.

THE FATHER OF HER BABY *by Joanna Neil*

It had been a struggle, but Bethany wouldn't change a thing about her life. She has a rewarding job as a GP and an adorable son, Sam. But now Connor Broughton was back in town. Should she tell him about her baby? In the end he found out on his own — and asked the one question she didn't want to answer: who was Sam's father?

On sale 6th September 2002

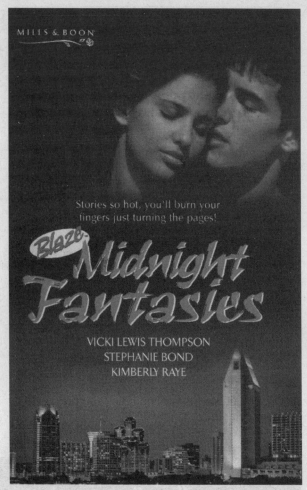

FREE!

2 Books
and a surprise gift!

We would like to take this opportunity to thank you for reading this Mills & Boon® book by offering you the chance to take TWO more specially selected titles from the Medical Romance™ series absolutely FREE! We're also making this offer to introduce you to the benefits of the Reader Service™ —

- ★ FREE home delivery
- ★ FREE gifts and competitions
- ★ FREE monthly Newsletter
- ★ Books available before they're in the shops
- ★ Exclusive Reader Service discount

Accepting these FREE books and gift places you under no obligation to buy; you may cancel at any time, even after receiving your free shipment. Simply complete your details below and return the entire page to the address below. *You don't even need a stamp!*

YES! Please send me 2 free Medical Romance books and a surprise gift. I understand that unless you hear from me, I will receive 4 superb new titles every month for just £2.55 each, postage and packing free. I am under no obligation to purchase any books and may cancel my subscription at any time. The free books and gift will be mine to keep in any case.

M2ZEB

Ms/Mrs/Miss/Mr ....Initials..
BLOCK CAPITALS PLEASE

Surname..

Address...

....

....Postcode ....

Send this whole page to:
UK: The Reader Service, FREEPOST CN8I, Croydon, CR9 3WZ
EIRE: The Reader Service, PO Box 4546, Kilcock, County Kildare (stamp required)

Offer not valid to current Reader Service subscribers to this series. We reserve the right to refuse an application and applicants must be aged 18 years or over. Only one application per household. Terms and prices subject to change without notice. Offer expires 29th November 2002. As a result of this application, you may receive offers from other carefully selected companies. If you would prefer not to share in this opportunity please write to The Data Manager at the address above.

Mills & Boon® is a registered trademark owned by Harlequin Mills & Boon Limited.
Medical Romance™ is being used as a trademark.